The SPRING Duchess

A Duchess for All Seasons
Book Two

JILLIAN EATON

This is a work of fiction. Names, characters, places and incidents are either the product of the author's imagination or are used fictitiously, and any resemblance to actual persons, living or dead, business establishments, events, or locales is entirely coincidental.

© 2018 by Jillian Eaton
ISBN: 9781980865537

www.jillianeaton.com

All rights reserved. Except for use in any review, the reproduction or utilization of this work in whole or in part in any form is forbidden without the written permission of the author.

*A **BLINDING FLASH OF LIGHTNING ILLUMINATED** the duke's countenance, and even though it only lasted for a split second it was long enough for Eleanor to see the dark desire in Derek's gaze. Her breath caught in her throat as he prowled towards her, his steps long and fluid like a panther, his ebony hair just as sleek and his eyes...his eyes glowing with a feral intensity she'd never seen before.*

"What – what are you doing?" she asked, swallowing nervously. A quick glance over her shoulder revealed there was nowhere for her to go as he advanced with a single-minded purpose. In four strides she was pinned against the chaise longue, the back of her knees pushing against the sumptuous velvet as she leaned away from him.

"Something I should have done a long time ago."

"K-kiss me?" she ventured.

His grin was nothing shy of wicked. "That's a good place to start."

As thunder boomed and lightning flashed, Derek buried his hands in her unruly waterfall of auburn curls, tilted her head back, and plundered her mouth with his...

Prologue

"Hopeless," Mrs. Ascot declared flatly. "Absolutely hopeless."

As she watched her daughter flounce about the room in something that vaguely resembled a waddle (but looked nothing like a waltz), Lady Ward was forced to agree. Eleanor was a sweet-natured girl. Always happy, if a bit too optimistic at times. Pretty, if one didn't mind orange hair and freckles. And absolutely, positively, *horrendously* hopeless.

"Ellie, dear, that's enough," she called out, waving her gloved hand like a white flag of surrender in the hopes of catching her daughter's attention before she twisted her ankle and fell into the pianoforte. Or knocked over the bookshelf. Or sent the tea service crashing to the floor.

The first time Eleanor's clumsiness had revealed itself Lady Ward had attributed it to an uneven floorboard. The second time she'd blamed the wind (even though every window in the drawing room had been tightly closed). But when it happened a third time she was forced to admit that maybe, just maybe, the fault lay with Eleanor. Wanting a second opinion before her daughter's debut into high society, she'd immediately sent for Mrs. Ascot, an old friend from boarding school who now ran a distinguished training academy for young debutantes. If anyone could help Ellie, it was Mrs. Ascot.

"There is a girl in my class with a wooden leg who moves more gracefully than your daughter," Mrs. Ascot declared. Her thin black eyebrows lifted a fraction of an inch when Eleanor began to flounce about in a circle, her arms waving madly in the air. "Send for a doctor at once, Helena. The poor thing is having a seizure."

Lady Ward really shouldn't have laughed, but it was either that or dissolve into a puddle of tears, and when had tears ever solved anything? "I – I believe she is attempting a simple rotation. I'm sure if she had a partner it would look more seemly."

"Nothing could make what your daughter is doing appear seemly." The corners of Mrs. Ascot's stern mouth tightened into a disapproving frown. "I'm sorry, Helena. Truly I am. But there is nothing I can do."

"Oh, but surely there is *something*."

"Do you want my advice?"

"Yes." Lady Ward nodded so enthusiastically her lace cap almost flew off her head. "Yes, *please*. I know

Ellie may seem a bit rough around the edges, but she really is a lovely girl. It's just that dancing…well, as you can see dancing is not one of her strengths."

"What *are* some of her strengths?" Mrs. Ascot asked bluntly.

Lady Ward smiled gamely. "There are almost too many to list, I'm afraid. She's always had a brilliant head for numbers. Just brilliant. And she *loves* to read. Lord Ward has always said that if you are looking for Ellie just find the nearest book, and there she'll be! She also has a great affinity for animals, and is a skilled rider."

"What about the gentle arts? Painting? Singing? What instrument does she prefer?"

"Well…ah…You see, her pursuits have always been a bit more *academic* in nature."

Mrs. Ascot's frown deepened. "It almost sounds as if Eleanor is a bluestocking."

"No, no, no" Lady Ward said, horrified at the very idea. "Certainly not!"

"I sympathize with you, Helena. Truly. But there is nothing I can do. Sometimes we must simply accept someone for who they are…and who they are not. Your daughter is not destined for a great match, but perhaps with a bit of luck she might find a suitable widower or the third son of a baron."

"The – the third son of a *baron*?" Lady Ward

sputtered. "Surely she can do better than that!"

Unfortunately, Eleanor chose that precise moment to lose her balance and fall back into the curtains. With a muffled shriek her feet flew up above her head and she disappeared into the heavy drapes. Lady Ward smiled weakly at Mrs. Ascot.

"So sorry to have wasted your time. Let me see you out."

"ARE THEY GONE, HENNY?" Waiting until the sound of disappointed footsteps had faded away, Eleanor untangled herself from the curtains and carefully scooped Mrs. Hensworth, her beloved pet hedgehog, out of her pocket.

She'd found the little insectivore – contrary to popular belief, hedgehogs were *not* rodents – in the garden stuck in the bottom of a pot. The victim of an attack from above, the little hedgehog had been missing a large chunk of her quills. After nursing her back to health, Eleanor had attempted to release her back into the garden. But Henny (having grown fond of warm milk and blueberry scones) had stubbornly refused to leave her pocket. She'd become Eleanor's first pet, but not the last. Unbeknownst to her parents, Eleanor had quite the menagerie living in the old garden shed behind their townhouse.

Her beloved collection of orphaned animals, all of

which required her daily attention, was one of the main reasons she'd just made an utter fool of herself in front of Mrs. Ascot. The last thing in the world she wanted was to be shipped off to some training academy for distinguished young women! Eleanor wasn't distinguished. She was *happy*. And she saw no reason why her entire life should have to change just because she was now a debutante.

Debutante.

How she hated that word! Up until two months ago she'd only heard it a couple of times. Now it felt as though it were being thrown in her face every time she turned around.

"Debutantes do not slouch."

"Debutantes do not eat in the stables."

"Debutantes do not read during supper."

"Debutantes do not speak unless spoken to."

Frustrated beyond all bearing, she'd demanded to know what a debutante *could* do. And she'd gotten a very unwelcome glimpse at the future that awaited her when her mother had promptly replied, *'Marry well, Ellie. A debutante can marry well.'*

Well, she didn't want to marry well. In fact, she didn't want to marry at all!

"What do you think, Henny?" Lifting the hedgehog up to her face, she kissed the tip of Henny's twitchy nose. "Do you think my life should be defined by a man? Because I don't. Men are useless, dimwitted clods who–"

"ELLIE!" Lady Ward's shrill voice rang through the entire downstairs. With a heavy sigh, Eleanor slipped Henny back into her pocket and prepared herself to face the music. Or in this case, the disappointment of a loving mother who genuinely wanted the best for her daughter…but was going about it in a very convoluted way.

"Yes, Mother?" she said when Lady Ward marched into the drawing room and regarded her only daughter with an expression torn between affection and exasperation. A kind-faced woman with hair several shades darker and straighter than Eleanor's fiery red curls, Helena Ward had been regarded as a Great Beauty during her debut and time had done little to detract from her loveliness. An opinionated daughter who refused to adhere to the rules of Society, however, had begun to take a noticeable toll.

There were more lines around the corners of her mouth than there had been six months ago. Lines from frowning when Eleanor said something particularly outlandish. Lines from wincing when she tripped over something. Lines from shouting out in surprise when a little hedgehog went scurrying across the hall. Lines from staying awake at night with her mouth pinched in a tight line of worry as she fretted over Eleanor's future prospects. For who would possibly want an outspoken girl who defied convention at every turn? A girl who would rather have her head in the stars than her feet planted firmly on the ground. A girl who had more pets than friends – she knew *all* about the garden shed – and who didn't know a waltz from a quadrille?

"I am sorry to say that Mrs. Ascot cannot offer her support at this time." With a loud, somewhat dramatic sigh Lady Ward collapsed into the nearest chair and brought the back of her hand to her temple. "She wanted me to extend her regrets, and to let you know that she is simply too busy."

"Oh, she isn't busy." Eleanor rolled her eyes. "She simply doesn't want her name attached to a complete and utter disaster."

"You're not a disaster!" Lady Ward protested. "Well, not a complete one anyways."

"Thank you."

"But I *do* wish you would try, Ellie," said Lady Ward, gazing up at her daughter beseechingly. "I realize coordination is not your strong suit, but surely you can manage a simple waltz without doing yourself bodily harm."

Seeing the strain in the corners of her mother's eyes, Eleanor felt a twinge of guilt. "Maybe I could have tried a *little* harder," she admitted. "But I fail to see how dancing is an accurate reflection of one's character.

Instead of balls, wouldn't it be better if potential couples sat around a library and discussed famous literary works or current events or the most recent scientific discoveries?"

"Why ever would they do that?" Lady Ward asked, sounding genuinely confused.

"Because those are *real* things that effect our *real* lives. Dancing is…dancing is superfluous."

Lady Ward gasped. "Eleanor Rose, watch your tongue!"

"I'm sorry Mother, but it's true. Furthermore–"

"Please," her mother grimaced. "No more lectures on the inequality of women and their inferior status in Society. I feel a headache coming on."

"I wasn't going to lecture," Eleanor lied. "I was just going to ask why men are allowed, even encouraged, to show off their mental and physical prowess in a variety of ways while women are expected to be silent and well behaved? We're not vases meant to sit up on a shelf and be admired from afar. I don't want to collect dust, Mother. I want to do what makes me *happy*. Life is far too short to be miserable."

"I fail to see why you could not be perfectly happy as a viscount's wife," Lady Ward sniffed. "Mayhap even an earl if you really apply yourself. I'm happy, aren't I? And I've been married to your father for twenty-four years."

"Yes," Eleanor conceded. "You are very happy, and it pleases me to see you so. But I'm not you, Mother."

"Don't I know it," Lady Ward muttered under her breath.

"What was that?" Eleanor said suspiciously.

"Nothing, dear." She smiled fondly at her daughter. "Look at you. You're a vision, Ellie. Any man would be lucky to have you. We simply have to find one willing to overlook your…quirks. There are dozens of eligible men this Season. How hard could it possibly be?"

Chapter One

Five Failed Seasons Later...

"If you tread on my foot one more time," Eleanor said pleasantly, "my hedgehog is going to bite you."

His eyes widening, Lord Stanhope, an earl of considerably good wealth and breeding, stopped abruptly in his tracks. "I'm sorry, I fear I must have misheard you. Did you say – did you say *hedgehog*?"

"I am happy to report that your hearing is much better than your dancing, my lord. I did indeed say 'my hedgehog'." Taking advantage of Lord Stanhope's temporary paralysis due to the absurdity of his partner claiming she had a pest in her pocket, Eleanor wrenched her hands free of his sweaty grasp and carefully pulled Henny out of the pocket she'd had fashioned in her ball gown specifically for her tiny little friend.

"This is Henny," she said, holding the hedgehog aloft. "She's curled in a ball right now because she is sleeping, but I can assure you that when she is awake her teeth are quite sharp and capable of doing considerable damage, as are her quills."

"You – you have a *rodent* in your dress," Lord Stanhope said, looking positively aghast. Eleanor's eyes narrowed.

"Henny is not a rodent, she is an insectivore. It's a common mistake, however if you look closely at the tip of her nose–"

"You're mad. Absolutely barmy." Lord Stanhope backed so quickly away that he bumped into another couple. "She has a rat!" he yelled, jabbing his finger at Eleanor and poor Henny, who had been roused by all the noise and was blinking drowsily in confusion. "She has a rat in her pocket!"

"Oh for heaven's sake," Eleanor said crossly. "I just told you, Henny is not a rodent, she's an insectivore."

"Is that a *mouse*?" a woman in green muslin screeched.

"Don't be silly. Why on earth would I bring a mouse to a ball? Henny is a hedgehog. Can't you see her quills?" But the damage had already been done, and as every head within twenty feet of Eleanor swiveled, she quickly slipped Henny back into her pocket and made a mad dash for the nearest exit, not caring who she had to shove out of her way to get there. She vaguely heard her mother calling her name, but not wanting to linger among the close-minded flock of arrogant pigeons a second longer she opened the first door she came across and immediately shut it behind her.

Red-faced and perspiring, Eleanor dabbed at her forehead with a handkerchief as she walked swiftly down a carpeted hallway and into an empty parlor. The fireplace was dormant and only a single candle glowed in the window, making it the perfect shadowy hideout. The faint scent of cigar smoke lingered in the air, revealing she hadn't been the first person to find a quiet reprieve in the room, but that did not matter as long as she was the last. Exhaling a long, deep breath she hadn't even realized she'd been holding, she sat down on a plush velvet settee and, after a bit of coaxing, managed to draw a rather disgruntled Henny back out into the open.

"I'm sorry," she apologized as she sat the hedgehog on her lap. "I know you don't like loud noises, but I was afraid to leave you in my room. Not with that mean old tomcat lurking about."

Eleanor and her mother were currently guests of Lord and Lady Hanover at their estate just outside of London. They'd arrived two days ago with plans to stay for a fortnight, but once Henny's presence became widely known Eleanor would not be surprised if their invitation was revoked before the night was out.

"Blast and damn," she muttered, borrowing one of her father's favorite curses. As ill at ease with social gatherings as his daughter, Lord Ward had remained at home, citing 'business meetings' that he needed to attend. Which was complete balderdash, of course, but since he was a man – and head of the household – he got to do what he wished while she, a lowly woman and daughter, had to obey whatever directive she was given.

It simply wasn't *fair*. But then nothing ever was, particularly if you were female.

"I don't understand why the lot of us don't revolt, Henny." Absently stroking a hand down the hedgehog's prickly back – being mindful to pat in the direction of the quills – she stared hard at a painting above the mantle. "We bear the children, don't we? Without us men would quite literally be nonexistent. And yet they control the money, and the politics, and the titles, and the laws. It's absurd. Don't you think?"

It was impossible to decipher the mind of a hedgehog, of course, but she took Henny's quiet snuffle as a sign of concurrence.

"I knew you would agree with me. No one else does. They think I'm strange and my ideas eccentric." Her gaze fell to her lap as an odd tightness overcame her throat. "And Mother wonders why no one has offered for my hand," she muttered.

This time Henny purred, and the contented sound made Eleanor smile. No matter what the circumstances, her animals could always be counted on to lift her spirits. Which was why she planned to take the entire lot of them and move to the country when her third Season came to the same disappointing conclusion as all the rest.

She'd recently struck up a correspondence with an elderly aunt in Hampshire whose husband had passed over the winter. Aunt Biddy was in desperate need of a strong, able-bodied person to help care for her cottage and the surrounding land. Lady Ward had been trying to coax Aunt Biddy to London, but the old woman was stubborn and set in her ways. She refused to leave the place she'd called home for nearly six decades, and eventually Lady Ward had thrown up her hands.

'If she won't come to us, then there's nothing else we can do'.

But that wasn't precisely true, was it? As it turned out, Aunt Biddy's stubbornness wasn't the only trait she and her niece had in common. They both loved animals, and Aunt Biddy had agreed to house Eleanor *and* her menagerie in exchange for help around the farm. It would be hard work, she'd warned, but Eleanor wasn't afraid to get her hands dirty. What scared her more was keeping them pristinely clean.

All she needed to do was get through one more Season with her sanity intact. If the little incident with Lord Stanhope was any indication it was going to be a challenge, but with an end in sight Eleanor was more than ready to rise to the occasion.

"I'll be a spinster living in the country," she told Henny happily. "Can you think of anything more divine?" For most women a reclusive life far from the glittering ballrooms of London would have been their worst nightmare, but for Eleanor it was a dream come true.

Now the only thing she needed to do was tell her mother.

"But that can wait, can't it?" Setting Henny down on the sofa when the little hedgehog began to wiggle, she leaned her head back and closed her eyes, a light smile gracing her lips as she imagined all of the ways her life would change for the better once she was free from the constraints of High Society.

There would be no more balls. Or ball gowns, for that matter. No more dancing. No more struggling to make polite conversation when all she wanted to do was discuss Sir William Horrocks' latest invention, a variable speed batton that was going to revolutionize the power loom. No more hiding Henny in her pocket. Speaking of which…

"Ouch!" she exclaimed when she felt a sharp tug at the top of her head. Blindly reaching up to her hair, she gave a very unladylike curse when her fingers accidentally brushed against Henny's prickly quills. With an alarmed squeal the hedgehog scurried down the side of the sofa and plopped onto the floor.

A beam of moonlight reflected off the shiny object Henny carried in her mouth as she scooted under a table and disappeared from sight. A shiny object that looked suspiciously like one of Eleanor's diamond encrusted hairpins.

"Not *another* one!" she moaned. If she lost one more hairpin her mother would never let her go live with Aunt Biddy. "Henny, you damned thief, get back here this instant!"

Dropping to her hands and knees she tried to follow the hedgehog under the table, but of course she didn't fit. Derriere in the air and face pressed to the ground, she squinted one eye closed as she searched for Henny underneath a chaise longue. The parlor was well appointed and there were dozens of places a hedgehog could hide, which meant if she was going to retrieve her beloved pet she needed to do it quickly. Once Henny found a soft place to burrow into there was no telling *when* she would come out. Last year at Lady Markham's dinner party she'd disappeared for nearly five hours!

Lady Ward had been thrilled when Eleanor had requested to stay longer. She'd thought her daughter wanted to spend more time with a viscount, but in reality Eleanor had needed the extra time to look for Henny. She'd eventually found her in the kitchens stuffed inside a bread box happily munching on day old crumpets, but there was no telling where she'd gotten off to this time.

"Henny! Oh Henny, please come back. I'm not cross with you. I promise." Eleanor started to back out from underneath the table, but with a gasp of dismay she realized her dress was caught. She pulled a bit harder and was met with a sharp tearing sound. Oh dear. A lost hairpin was *nothing* compared to a ruined gown, particularly one that had cost as much as this.

Balancing crookedly on one elbow, she tried to peer behind her to see what she was snagged on, but her awkward position made it impossible to see past her voluminous skirts. Suffice it to say she was stuck. Stuck with her rump up in the air and her head under a table.

"Well this is a fine pickle. Henny, I've changed my mind. I *am* cross with you. *Very* cross." But if the mischievous hedgehog heard – or cared – she gave no indication, and Eleanor struck her fist against the floor in frustration.

What was she going to *do*? Wait until someone found her, she supposed. And pray that someone was a maid and not a gossipy old hen who would gleefully spread the news of her embarrassing predicament far and wide. There was always the possibility her mother would come looking for her. All things considered, that was probably the best scenario. At least she knew Lady

Ward would never whisper a word of this to anyone. In fact, she would probably demand the entire thing be stricken from both of their memories, just like the time Eleanor had jumped into a pond at Hyde Park in an attempt to rescue a floundering gosling.

'We will never *speak of this again,'* Lady Ward had furiously hissed as she'd draped her cloak around her daughter's shoulders before quickly ushering her into their carriage.

And they hadn't.

But it wasn't Lady Ward who stepped into the parlor.

Nor was it Lady Ward's voice that sent shivers of alarm rippling down Eleanor's spine.

"Well, well, well," a deep, husky masculine tone drawled. "What do we have here?"

Chapter Two

Derek despised balls.

Not his own, of course. He was quite fond of his own. But the balls that required a man to truss himself up like a stuffed goose and parade about the room like a preening peacock looking for a mate…*those* he hated. Which begged the question why the devil he was standing in the middle of a ball room. But as the answer was too convoluted to dissect without an entire bottle of brandy at the ready – and sadly no such brandy was available – he was instead possessed of a single-minded focus to do his duty and get the hell out as quickly as possible.

Sweeping his dance partner effortlessly across the marble floor, he turned a deaf ear to her endless prattle – why were women under the impression that waltzing required a steady flow of conversation? – and kept one eye on the massive long-case clock in the corner of the room.

In just a few short minutes it would strike midnight,

and when it did his evening promised to become much more titillating. For somewhere in the Hanover's massive estate his mistress was waiting…and she wasn't wearing any drawers.

Their little game of cat and mouse was one of the only reasons Derek had bothered to attend tonight. Well, that and he needed to keep up the pretense of looking for a wife to satisfy the terms of his grandfather's last will and testament. The scheming old bastard had enjoyed making his heir jump through hoops when he'd been alive, and nothing had changed after his death. To say their relationship had been tumultuous would have been like saying England had had a tiny little spat with France. In short, they'd despised one another. And the late Duke of Hawkridge had done everything in his power to ensure Derek would be miserable long after he was gone.

When the music dwindled and the waltz ended, Derek bowed neatly in front of his partner before excusing himself. Ignoring the volley of longing stares aimed at his back, he moved swiftly through the crowd, stopping only to select two glasses of champagne before abandoning the loud, sweltering ball room for the blessed quiet of a long hallway.

Lord Hanover's thick browed ancestors peered down at him from gilt framed paintings as he strolled through the palatial estate, occasionally stopping to open a door and peer inside. His anticipation built with every empty room he encountered until his loins were all but throbbing with need, and when he came across a parlor – and the curvy little arse sticking straight up in the air like a red flag in front of a very randy bull – he wasted no time in locking the door behind him and setting the champagne down so he could unbutton his jacket.

"Well, well, well." Dropping the jacket onto the back of a chair, he began to loosen his cravat. "What do we have here?"

The first time he'd seen Lady Vanessa he had been immediately captivated by her beauty. A willowy blonde with ice blue eyes, plump red lips, and features so delicate they might have been spun from glass, she was the epitome of a classic English rose. Yet while her physical appearance was what had initially piqued his interest, it was the seductive gleam of naughtiness in her gaze that kept it.

Derek had always been a man in possession of…darker appetites. And Vanessa, for all she might have looked and acted like a proper lady when out in public, was only too happy to feed his baser instincts when they were in private.

Her myriad of talents in the bedroom, coupled with the fact that she was already married and as such had no ridiculous illusions about becoming the next Duchess of Hawkridge, made her the perfect mistress.

Vanessa gave a tiny, indecipherable squeak of alarm as he approached her from behind and his desire deepened. Of all the roles she'd played a damsel in distresses had never been among them, and he was looking forward to how far she would carry it out. Although he wasn't quite certain why she was on the floor with her head under a table.

"I hope you're not wearing anything under those skirts," he said silkily as he crouched behind her and began to slide his hand up her calf. "Or else I'm going to have to – *bollocks*!"

Without warning Vanessa kicked back with all the strength and temerity of a mule, the heel of her slippered foot striking precariously close to his nether regions. Cursing, he scrambled back onto the sofa, both hands draped protectively over his cock and balls. A few inches higher…

"If this is some sort of new game, I fail to see the appeal," he said darkly.

"Game?" An outraged female voice that was decidedly *not* Vanessa's rose up from underneath the table. "This isn't a game, you overreaching oaf! How *dare* you touch me in such a familiar manner!"

"I…" Quick witted with a dagger sharp tongue, Derek rarely found himself at a loss for words. But as he stared down at the shapely derriere that belonged to someone other than his mistress, he couldn't think of a single thing to say. "I...I..."

"I, I, I," the impertinent voice mocked. "Why not try an apology, or better yet an explanation? Or are you such a rogue and a rake that you greet every woman you come across by running your hand up her leg?"

The chit was in a dark room wedged halfway beneath a table and she wanted an explanation from *him*? Eyes narrowing, Derek shot to his feet.

"I do apologize," he said stiffly. "I...thought you were someone else."

"You thought I was someone *else*?" the voice scoffed. "Pray tell, who else do you know who has her head stuck under a table?"

"I think the better question is what *you* are doing with your head stuck under a table."

"Clearly I am looking for something."

Clearly.

"And what would that something be?" he asked. "A lost earring? A necklace? Your dignity?"

"If you must know I am looking for Henny."

Confused, his gaze swept the room, but unless there was someone hiding behind the curtains they were the parlor's only two occupants. "Is Henny a pint-sized elf?"

"Do not be ridiculous. Henny is a hedgehog."

Of course she was. Because the only thing stranger than encountering a woman with her head stuck underneath a table was a woman with her head stuck underneath the table looking for her pet hedgehog.

"I wish you luck in your search," he said brusquely before he walked around the sofa and picked up his jacket. He was halfway to the door when the panic in the unknown woman's voice gave him pause.

"Wait!" she cried. "You can't just *leave*. You have to help me."

"Do I?" One dark brow lifted as he turned around. "And why would you require the help of a – what was it? Oh, yes. An 'overreaching oaf'? Don't worry, I am not a complete cad. I'll send for help."

"No, you can't!" She said it so quickly that the corners of his mouth twitched despite his annoyance at having been kicked, mocked, and insulted. In the span of a few seconds his mysterious assailant had done what no other woman – or man, for that matter – had ever dared. He should have left her to her fate without a second thought. And yet…

With a loud, irritated sigh, he dropped his jacket and rolled up his sleeves. "I suppose this can be my good deed for the year. What are you stuck on?"

"If I knew that then I wouldn't be stuck now, would I?" she replied tartly.

Saucy little wench. He was looking forward to hearing her stuttering apology when she realized just whom she'd been speaking to in such a disrespectful manner.

"Do not kick me again," he ordered as he crouched beside her and began to feel along the table for any sharp edges her gown could have gotten snagged on.

"What are you doing?" She craned her head around, offering him a glimpse of wide green eyes and thick curls the color of smoldering fire. He'd never cared for red hair. It was too bold. Too messy. Too temperamental. Vanessa's cold beauty was much more to his liking.

"Hold still." His fingers bumped against a piece of scrollwork on the edge of the table. At some point the scrollwork must have come loose for a nail had been used to secure it, and it was the nail head that had caught the woman's dress. "I've almost got it – *bollocks*," he cursed under his breath when the fabric slipped from his grasp. "I thought I told you to hold still!"

"I *am* holding still."

"No," he said through clenched teeth. "You're not. This blasted sofa is in the way. I'm going to have to straddle you."

"You're going to have to – *what are you doing?*" she yelped when he mounted her backside as one would a mare, muscular thighs gently squeezing her slender hips. From this position he was finally able to get a firm grip on the nail...and his grip wasn't the only thing that was firm. For such a bristly little thing she was certainly soft in all the places that counted.

He was half-tempted to explore more of those soft places, but not fancying another kick in the groin he ignored his misplaced arousal (for he knew the woman his body *really* desired was Vanessa), and quickly got to work on the nail. Unfortunately, in a twist of horribly bad timing, no sooner had he pried the dress free than the parlor door suddenly swung open.

"Eleanor?" a lady's shrill voice rang out. "Eleanor, are you in – *oh*! I am so sorry, I did not mean to...Eleanor? Eleanor, is that you?"

Derek willed the redhead to remain silent. They may have been fully clothed, but their current position didn't exactly lend itself to innocence. Surely she knew what would happen to her reputation if she was discovered kneeling beneath a man in the dark confines of a parlor. But apparently she either didn't know, or she didn't care, and he inwardly cringed when she promptly responded with a cheerful, "Yes Mother! It's me."

"Now you've bloody well done it," he growled as he swung his leg over and stalked to the far side of the sofa, bracing his hand on the wooden armrest. But he knew no matter how much distance he put between them, it would never be enough. The damage, such as it was, had already been done.

Now that she was no longer stuck, the redhead –

Eleanor – quickly backed out from beneath the table and stood up. Innocent green eyes, flecked with gold and framed by thick auburn lashes, met his. There was a smattering of freckles across her nose and cheeks, like cinnamon dusted on the top of a queen cake. He was suddenly filled with the nearly irrepressible urge to brush his thumb across her face and see if the freckles would melt away beneath his touch. A peculiar urge, as he was not an affectionate man. But then this had been a most peculiar evening.

"What have I done?" Eleanor asked, her brows knitting with confusion.

"What have you done?" His laugh was flat and humorless as his calculating gaze flicked to the woman who remained frozen in front of the door. At least she'd had the presence of mind to close it behind her, but rumors had a way of slipping through even the smallest of cracks. Rumors that would ruin him as surely as they would ruin Eleanor. If not for that wretched will…

"You've damned us both," he said grimly. "That's what you've done."

Chapter Three

Eleanor was not surprised to discover the man who had grudgingly helped her was handsome. If there was one thing she'd learned over the past six Seasons, it was that arrogant men tended towards handsomeness. A pity, really. All those chiseled jaws and thick hair and strong chins wasted on conceited scoundrels who falsely believed they were superior to their peers because of their physical appearance, when in fact it was the inside of a person that mattered most.

Her scowling rescuer was tall and broad-shouldered with black hair swept back from a high, smooth temple and side whiskers that extended all the way down past his ears. He had distinct, evenly spaced features and a perfectly well-shaped mouth that was ruined by a frown. His eyes were the color of rich dark brandy, the sort her father kept high on the shelf in crystal decanters and only drank on very special occasions. A wide chest tapered down to a narrow waist and then widened into muscular thighs enclosed in fawn colored breeches. Eleanor's cheeks pinkened when she remembered how those thighs had clenched around her hips, and she abruptly diverted her gaze to her mother.

"I'm sorry I was gone so long. I was looking for Henny, you see, and then I became stuck under the – what is it?" she asked when Lady Ward began to vehemently shake her head from side to side. "What's wrong? Are you ill? You didn't eat the shrimp, did you? Because you know what happens when you eat shrimp."

"Oh Eleanor," Lady Ward cried, clasping her gloved hands beneath her chin. "What have you *done*?"

Eleanor's fair brow creased. Why was everyone under the impression she'd done something? Other than threatening to turn Henny loose on Lord Stanhope – no less than he'd deserved for nearly crippling her with his clumsy feet – she'd been on her best behavior for the entire evening. She hadn't brought up a single new invention over dinner or made an embarrassment of herself while dancing. Yes, she'd gotten stuck under a table…but that wasn't *her* fault. What was she supposed to have done? Just leave Henny in the parlor to her own devices? Speaking of which…

"Henny!" Her eyes widened. "I still need to find her."

"Will you forget about that damn animal for one moment! This is *serious*, Eleanor."

"You – you cursed." Shocked to her very core, Eleanor stared at her mother with her mouth agape. "You never curse."

"Yes, well, I've never walked in on my daughter in a compromising position with a man before either! I need to sit down," Lady Ward muttered, clutching her temple. "I'm feeling very faint. Black dots. There are black dots everywhere."

"Here." Moving with impressive speed, the man whose name Eleanor still did not know lifted a chair and placed it behind her mother. Then he rocked back on his heels, crossed his arms, and skewered her with a glare so frigid she felt the chill of it all the way across the room.

"Your chaperone is correct," he said. "This is serious. Someone of your age should have known better than to put herself in such a vulnerable position."

Eleanor blinked. She knew two and twenty wasn't considered young by any means, but she liked to think she had a few years left before she was sentenced to spinsterhood! Never mind that was precisely the sort of life she had in mind. But it was one thing to refer to herself as a spinster. Quite another when someone else did it, especially when that someone else was an overweening lord easily five years her senior!

"Someone of my age?" she replied indignantly. "What is that supposed to mean?"

"It means you are not a fresh-faced debutante, inasmuch as you possess the ignorance of one." One thick brow arched. "You should have known better than to have been alone in a room without a proper chaperone. You've ruined both of our lives, you stupid girl. And you don't even have the good sense to realize it."

If her jaw had dropped when her mother cursed, it positively sagged wide open now. But while most women would have burst into tears under the weight of such a crushing insult, Eleanor rose to the occasion like an Amazon strapping on her battle armor. Marching right up to her dark-eyed antagonist, she fearlessly jabbed a finger at the middle of his rock hard chest and snapped, "Better a stupid girl than an arrogant bounder whose head is so inflated it's a wonder it remains attached to your neck!"

"Eleanor!" Lady Ward gasped, looking up at her daughter with horror. "You cannot speak to his grace like that! Apologize at once!"

Her slim shoulders stiffening, Eleanor stepped back and frowned down at her mother. "I most certainly will not. Did you hear what he said to me?"

"Please darling," Lady Ward pleaded. "For once in your life, do as you are told." She lowered her voice and flicked an anxious glance over her shoulder to where the stranger stood with an oddly smug expression on his face, as if he were greatly anticipating whatever Lady Ward was about to say next. "Don't you have any idea whom you are speaking to? You have just insulted the *Duke* of Hawkridge. You simply *must* apologize."

So the conceited cad was a duke, was he? Well bully on that. It didn't matter if he was the King of England. A fancy title did not give him the right or the means to belittle her.

"I don't care who he is," she said, and was rewarded for her bold statement when the duke's smug smirk was abruptly replaced by a hard, narrow-eyed scowl. "I've done nothing but call a donkey a donkey." Her head tilted thoughtfully to the side. "Or in this case an ass an ass."

"Oh," Lady Ward moaned as she tipped forward and dropped her head between her knees. "The dots, the dots."

"Mother, you are not going to – Henny!" Eleanor cried with delight when she saw a tiny black nose peeking out from beneath the curtains. Scurrying over to the window, she snatched up her pet and quickly returned her to the safe confines of her pocket. The little hedgehog let out a squawk of protest before curling up into a ball and promptly falling asleep, no doubt exhausted by all of the excitement she'd caused. Turning back towards the middle of the parlor, Eleanor discovered her mother sadly shaking her head from side to side while the duke stared at her as if she'd suddenly sprouted a third arm.

"What the devil did you just put in your pocket?" he demanded.

"That was Henny. My hedgehog."

"You have a bloody *hedgehog*?"

Her lips thinned. "Have you listened to anything I've said?"

"I've done my best not to," he drawled, an insufferable smirk toying with the corners of his mouth.

Odious man. One would think a duke would possess better manners. Then again, she couldn't exactly say she was surprised. Her sixth Season nearly completed and she'd yet to meet a *single* lord who was tolerable enough to engage in conversation for longer than five minutes. Presumptuous swine, the lot of them. And this one was no different from the rest.

"Now that I have found Henny, I am no longer in need of your services." She gave a vague sweep of her arm, dismissing him as if he were nothing more than a lowly footman. But he didn't leave. Instead, much to her general annoyance, he addressed her mother.

"Might I have the pleasure of learning your name, my lady?"

"Lady Ward, Your Grace," said Eleanor's mother with a tight, uneasy smile that furrowed her brow. "Lady Helena Ward."

"Lady Ward." The duke bowed, and Eleanor rolled her eyes. "I am sorry to make your acquaintance under such…straining circumstances. But I should very much like you to believe me when I say that absolutely nothing untoward happened between your daughter and me, despite what it may have looked like. However, let it be known I do realize the gravity of the situation at hand, as well as the fate that awaits your daughter should any word of this ever escape the room."

"Of course nothing untoward happened," Eleanor burst out. "I'd rather kiss Mr. Haybeak!"

Mr. Haybeak was her pet duck.

"Eleanor, be quiet," Lady Ward snapped. "Let His Grace speak."

"Why should he be allowed to talk while I–"

"*Eleanor.*"

"Fine," she grumbled. "Henny and I will be over here." Giving her pocket a reassuring pat, she retreated to the far corner of the parlor and pretended to look at the leather bound books lining the shelves.

"Please let me apologize on behalf of my daughter, Your Grace. She has always been headstrong. I fear her father and I did not do enough to curb her willfulness when she was a child, and she has carried that willful nature into adulthood."

Eleanor bit back a snort as she pulled a book off the shelf and began to flip through the pages. In a society where tenacity and intelligence were frowned upon while docility and obedience were encouraged, she was *glad* to be in a possession of a willful nature.

"I can see that, Lady Ward. Your daughter is certainly…unique."

"Thank you," Lady Ward said, even though it was obvious the duke had not been paying a compliment.

"I take it she is unmarried?" he asked.

The book bobbled in Eleanor's hand. Why would a duke care if she was wed or not?

"Yes, Your Grace. Although not for lack of offers. My daughter is very particular."

This time Eleanor couldn't quite silence her snort in time. The only *offer* she'd received had been from a baron old enough to be her grandfather. He'd passed away in his sleep before she'd been able to reject it.

"And she is not currently engaged?"

"No, Your Grace."

The duke sighed. It was a heavy sigh. The sort of sigh a man gave right before he stepped up to the gallows and stretched out his neck. "Then I am afraid I see no other recourse."

No other recourse? She didn't like the sound of that. She didn't like the sound of that one bit. "What are you–"

"I will marry your daughter, Lady Ward," said the duke, effectively rendering Eleanor absolutely and completely speechless for the first time in her entire life. "It is, after all, the only right thing to do."

Chapter Four

Lady Ward was crying.

Eleanor was shouting.

The hedgehog was chirping.

Ignoring all three of them, Derek went to the door and locked it, then angled a chair beneath the doorknob for good measure. No one was leaving the parlor until they had their bloody story straight. Desperately wishing he had a bottle of brandy at his disposal, he settled for draining the two flutes of champagne before he turned to face his reluctant (to put it mildly) fiancée and elated mother-in-law.

"Quiet." He snapped the word out with the same sharp tone he used for his hounds, and it had a similar effect. At least on Lady Ward and the hedgehog. Eleanor was far more difficult to subdue. Not that he was surprised. 'Willful nature' indeed. The chit was what nightmares were born of. And he was going to marry her.

Here's to you, Grandfather, he toasted silently as he

tipped one of the empty flutes up towards the ceiling. *Wherever you are, and we both know it isn't heaven, I know you're no doubt laughing your arse off, you old bastard.*

After twenty-three years of constantly being told he wasn't good enough, he wasn't man enough, he wasn't deserving enough to inherit a dukedom, Derek would be lying if he said he'd shed a tear over his grandfather's coffin. His grandfather may have raised him – his own mother and father had perished in a boating accident when he was eleven years old – but there'd been no love lost between the two men. His grandmother, a sweet woman who had always snuck him hard candies, said it was because they were too much alike. Whatever the reason, Derek had been relieved when the tyrannical goat had finally met his maker. Until his grandfather's solicitor had sat him down and explained the unusual terms of the late duke's will.

It was really quite simple, which made it all the more infuriating. Derek would immediately inherit the title and all of the land and properties that went along with it. But he would only *keep* the title and the land and properties if he married before his twenty-ninth birthday *and* (here was the crux of the bloody matter) managed to avoid any major scandals.

The will was a way for his grandfather to control him even in death, and despite seeking the counsel of no less than two dozen different solicitors, he'd yet to discover a way to overturn the damned thing. Yes, it was unusual and even possibly illegal, all of the solicitors had told him. But in order to fight it he would have to go to the courts which were notoriously slow and cumbersome. It could take years before they ruled in his favor, and in the meantime everything – from his townhouse in London to Hawkridge Castle in Surrey – would be placed under the temporary care of the Crown.

Given that he had no intention of pandering to King George every time he wanted use of his own bloody money, Derek had grudgingly accepted the terms of the will. All things considered, it actually hadn't been that bad. Mr. Evans, the solicitor in charge of making sure the terms of the will were met, was an annoying little fellow, but he'd stayed out of Derek's way for the most part. He still had an entire year left to find a bride, and by some small miracle he'd even managed to keep his nose clean of any scandals – until a certain redhead with an affinity for odd pets asked him to help free her from underneath a table.

"I still don't see why I have to marry him." Hands on her narrow hips, Eleanor shot Derek a look of such utter revulsion that he blinked. "Who cares what other people say? *I* know the truth, which is that nothing happened!"

Her brown eyes shining, Lady Ward wrapped her arms around her daughter and squeezed her tight. "My darling," she sniffled happily. "My sweet, darling girl. Do you know how proud of you I am?"

"For getting stuck under a table?" Eleanor said incredulously.

"Don't be absurd," Derek drawled. And because some perverse side of him liked it when her eyes flashed and her cheeks flushed with angry heat, he added, "Anyone can get stuck under a table. But it's a rare lady who gets to marry a duke."

There went her eyes and her cheeks, and he couldn't help but grin at how easy she was to antagonize. He felt like a young lad again tugging on Mindy Caterwaul's braids. Except that teasing had led to a kiss, whereas this was leading straight down the aisle.

"We're not married yet," Eleanor gritted out, glaring at him over her mother's shoulder. "Nor will we ever be! I could never marry *you*."

"Why not?" he asked, genuinely curious to hear her reasoning. Knowing he was the most eligible bachelor in all of England wasn't arrogance; it was simple fact. For years debutantes and their overbearing mothers had been trying to catch him, as if he were a prized trout to be hauled out of the water and displayed on their mantle. He'd managed to keep up the pretense of looking for a wife while simultaneously avoiding all of their advances. No small task, given the doggedness with which he'd been pursued. The Bow Street Runners were known far and wide as the best thief takers in all of London, but they were nothing compared to a desperate debutante.

Once he'd come home to find a young woman hiding behind one of his potted ferns. A potted fern, for the love of Christ! Thankfully his butler, a man accustomed to dealing with hysterical females, had managed to subdue the girl and send her on her way. Then there was the time he'd been accosted at the theatre. All he'd wanted to do was watch a bloody play in peace and quiet, but as soon as word got out that he was in one of the box seats absolute bedlam had ensued. He still had a mark on his arm where one lady's nails had dug a little too deep in her frantic attempt to cling to him as he'd made his exit.

Dangerous creatures, debutantes. Yet here was one – although to be fair, she *was* several years past her debut – that had managed, with the help of a runaway hedgehog and a sharp nail, to finally do what no other woman could: catch the Duke of Hawkridge. She should have been crying tears of joy along with her mother. Instead he was fairly certain that if she'd been in possession of a dagger she would have already tried to stab him with it.

Repeatedly.

"Why *not?*" Managing to slip free of her mother's embrace, Eleanor regarded him with wide eyes, her pink lips slightly parted and a faint wrinkle in the middle of her nose, as if she'd smelled something particularly distasteful. "For one thing, you're a pompous, self-entitled rake who has no regard for a woman's intelligence or her self-worth. You've spent your entire life being handed whatever you want, and it's turned you into a conceited, bullying–"

"All right," Derek growled, holding up his hand. "I get the bloody point. You don't want to marry me." Now it was *his* eyes that flashed. "Unfortunately, you don't have a choice in the matter."

"Of course I have a choice!" She lifted her chin defiantly. "And I choose *not* to marry you."

"Is that so?" he said in a very quiet, very gentle voice. Those who knew him understood that when he used such a tone it would be in their best interests to immediately flee in the opposite direction. Eleanor stepped closer.

"Yes," she said, meeting his hard gaze without flinching. "It is."

"In that case, I suppose you don't mind that if word of this gets out your reputation will be completely ruined and no man will ever have you?"

"First, word of this is never going to get out. Second–"

Derek harsh laugh cut her off. "Word *always* finds a way to get out, my lady. Even now I've no doubt there are busy bodies standing outside this room with their ears pressed to the door. Make no mistake, people *have* noted our absence. And it will not take very long for them to draw whatever dark conclusion they wish."

"Let them think what they want. Henny and I know the truth, and it doesn't matter a whit to me if my reputation is ruined."

"And your parents?" he challenged softly. "What of *their* reputation? For you can rest assured that they will be given the same cut direct as you. Your mother strikes me as a lovely, sociable woman. What a pity it will be when she's no longer received by any of her friends."

For the first time, Eleanor's courage faltered. "I...Mama?" she said uncertainly, looking back at Lady Ward. "That's not true, is it?"

"A scandal of this magnitude would indeed affect the entire family," Lady Ward said gravely. Then her expression softened. "But if you truly do not wish to marry His Grace, your father and I will not force you."

Eleanor's face was so easy to read Derek could decipher every emotion that flitted across her freckled countenance, from doubt to anger to disbelief, and finally, at long last, grim acceptance.

"Fine," she said shortly. "I'll marry you. But I'm *not* going to like it."

Derek smiled humorlessly. "That's fine, Red. Neither am I."

CHAPTER FIVE

Hawkridge Castle
(Almost) One Year Later

ELEANOR WARD had been married to the Duke of Hawkridge for eleven months, three days, and nine hours. In all that time, they had spoken exactly four sentences to one another.

Wait, she thought, a tiny line appearing between her winged eyebrows as she reconsidered. Was it four or was it five?

Five, she decided, if she counted the day of their wedding when he had looked into her eyes and said – albeit with great reluctance – "I do". Although did two words *really* count as an entire sentence?

Debatable.

"What do you think, Mr. Pumpernickel?" Coaxing

the white Persian up into her lap with a tiny sliver of anchovy, she scratched carefully under his chin, knowing the cat could go from purring to hissing in less time than it took to pour a cup of tea.

Not unlike her husband.

"Yes, you and the duke have quite a lot of traits in common, don't you? For one thing, you are both arrogant, not to mention quite unapproachable." Leaning back in her chair, she stared thoughtfully at the fireplace and the flames that hissed and crackled within. It may have been the first week of April, but Eleanor would hardly describe the weather as spring like.

The pond still had a thin crust of ice around the edges and the lawn was covered in a silvery blanket of frost. It was so cold the farmers had yet to plant their crops for the upcoming season, and whenever she went outside she was forced to bundle up as though it were the middle of January.

"You also come from impeccable bloodlines," she continued matter-of-factly. "Although you really have nothing to do with that. It wasn't as if you *chose* who you parents were going to be. How could you? You're a cat."

Mr. Pumpernickel's ears flattened.

"A brilliant cat," Eleanor assured him quickly. "Just brilliant."

Mr. Pumpernickel's tail swished.

"Oh, for heaven's sake. You're a genius. Second only to Socrates. There." She stroked a hand down his back. "Do you feel better?"

The Persian glared up at her from one slitted blue eye – he'd lost the other in a fight when he was only a kitten – before he jumped off her lap and trotted out of the parlor without so much as a backwards glance.

"Go on," she muttered under her breath. "I didn't want to speak to you anyways."

"Talking to yourself again?" Lady Georgiana Hanover glided into the room as if she were walking on a cloud. Sweeping her skirts to the side with an elegant flick of her wrist, she sat across from Eleanor and helped herself to one of the scones sitting on the glass table between them. "I thought we discussed that, darling," she said between nibbles.

"I wasn't talking to myself," Eleanor said defensively. "I was talking to Mr. Pumpernickel."

Georgiana lifted a sleek ebony brow. Like her brother, she had hair as dark as midnight and hazel eyes that stood out in startling contrast against her ivory countenance. Similar to the outside of a pearl, her skin had its own luminescent shine, something which Eleanor, with her scattering of freckles across sun kissed cheeks, was noticeably lacking.

"I do not think having a conversation with a cat is considered an improvement," she said haughtily. "We converse with *people*, Nora. Not empty rooms or persnickety felines."

"Mr. Pumpernickel is not persnickety. A touch arrogant, perhaps, but-"

"I did not come here to discuss the personality traits of your cat."

Eleanor's mouth set in a mulish frown. "Then why *are* you here?"

Try as she might - and she *had* tried - she'd yet to warm up to her husband's sister. It wasn't that Georgiana was mean, per say. It was just that they had absolutely nothing in common. Georgiana was fashionable and graceful and ladylike, while Eleanor was...well, none of those things. Put side by side, the two women couldn't have looked – or acted – more differently.

Georgiana, with her flawless style and stunning good looks, made Eleanor look like a country bumpkin with her disheveled hair and frumpy dresses that were more often than not smeared with dirt and grass stains after an afternoon spent frolicking outside with her animals. Neither one of them understood the other, and that misunderstanding had caused more than a few tensions since Georgiana's husband unexpectedly passed and she came to spend her mourning period at Hawkridge Castle.

Nestled amidst fifty thousand acres of rolling fields

to the east and thick, unharvested forest to the west, one would think Hawkridge Castle and its surrounding grounds would be large enough for two women to cohabitate in relative peace and harmony.

One would be wrong.

Constructed by her husband's great-great-great grandfather when Britain was still under the reign of the Tudors, the castle was massively sized…but apparently it wasn't *quite* big enough for Georgiana to mind her own business.

No matter which wing of the castle Eleanor tried to hide in (and there were plenty to choose from), her sister-in-law always managed to find her. She liked to pretend it was by accident. *"Oh, dear me!"* she would laugh, fluttering a hand over her chest. *"I didn't know you were in here."* But Eleanor had long ago begun to suspect she sought her out on purpose, like a dog hunting down a bone. And like a dog with a bone, she would use Eleanor to entertain herself for a time before reburying her and flitting away to do…well, whatever it was well bred, well behaved women did.

"I have some *very* exciting news to share." Draping her arm across the back of the chaise longue, Georgiana leaned back and delivered a smile that could only be described as glib. "Would you care to guess it?"

"No." Eleanor shook her head. "I really don't want to–"

"Oh, come on," Georgiana coaxed. "Don't be an old stick in the mud. I'll give you three guesses."

"I'm not being a stick in the mud, I just–"

"Nora." Beneath the sugary sweetness, her sister-in-law's voice was unmistakably sharp. "Be a dear and guess."

Since it would be easier – and quicker – to play along than to argue, Eleanor gritted her teeth and said, "You've decided to return to London."

Please, please, please let that be it.

"Return to town when I am still in mourning and the Season is nearly finished? Honestly, Nora, the way your mind works is quite amusing. Guess again!"

"You've bought a new hat?" she ventured.

"No." Georgiana's nose wrinkled. "It's as if you're not even trying."

"Fine. I give up." Grabbing a scone off the plate – her third of the morning – Eleanor stuffed the entire thing in her mouth so she wouldn't have to play Georgiana's ridiculous game to its conclusion.

"Oh Nora, you're so amusing," Georgiana said with an airy laugh. "And I must confess, I am *so* jealous of the way you can eat and eat and never gain a single stone. More than one of those scones and I need to let out my stays. They're just riddled with sugar and butter, you know."

They could have been filled with lard for all Eleanor

cared. Scones were delicious, and she'd be damned if she stopped eating them for something as frivolous as the size of her waistline. Although to be fair, her weight was never something she'd had to worry about. Not with all the energy she exerted caring for her menagerie of rescued animals.

While Georgiana spent her afternoons reading a book or working on her sewing, Eleanor was outside chasing after all manner of creatures, from the three goslings she'd found abandoned by their mother when she first arrived at Hawkridge to the litter of pygmy shrews she'd saved from the gardener's shovel.

After Mrs. Gibbons, the no nonsense housekeeper with a stern brow and even sterner tongue, made it clear that 'wild beasts' were *not* welcome inside, Eleanor had managed to coax the groundskeeper into allowing her use of the empty carriage barn. With the help of some footmen, she'd constructed half a dozen pens for her larger pets and four wooden box enclosures for those who still needed to be confined to a nest. For the most part the animals behaved themselves, but the goslings – now tripled in both size and temperament – had been proving particularly difficult as of late.

As soon as the ice was completely melted off the pond she was going to release them, but until then it was going to be a struggle to keep the young geese contained. The silly things insisted on following her wherever she went, and four days ago they'd nearly ended up on the dinner menu when they'd wandered into the kitchens and caused such a ruckus that Mrs. Gibbons had gone after them with a carving knife.

Poor Ronald had barely managed to escape with all of his feathers intact, and Donald had been one step away from being thrown straight into a pot of strew when Eleanor plucked him up and dashed outside. Mrs. Gibbons had been so furious that her entire face had turned a rather alarming shade of purple, and she *still* wasn't speaking to her. Eleanor may have been the duchess, but the housekeeper had made no attempts to disguise where her loyalties lay. She treasured Hawkridge Castle first and foremost, the duke second, Georgiana third, and Eleanor came in at a (very) distant fourth.

She didn't mind. She may have been married to the duke, but Georgiana was more of a duchess than she'd ever be. All of the servants deferred to her. When there was a decision to be made relating to the running of the household Georgiana made it, and Eleanor was only too happy to let her. It kept things at an even keel, and allowed her to do what she really wanted which was to care for her animals.

If not for the stone walls and thousands of acres of rolling fields and thick woods, she might as well have still been at home. She was married, but not married. A duchess, but not a duchess. It was a very peculiar position to be in, but one she'd adjusted to quite well over the past eleven months, three days, and – her gaze flicked to the mahogany table clock in the corner of the room – nine hours and twenty minutes. She did miss her parents on occasion, but they visited when they could and she and her mother exchanged monthly letters. One thing she did *not* miss?

Her husband.

It had been an enormous relief when the duke had informed her, in no uncertain terms, that they would lead completely separate lives once their vows were read.

"I am going to remain in London," he'd said, those brandy colored eyes of his daring her to challenge him. "And you will reside at Hawkridge Castle in Surrey."

"Do you mean we're going to live apart?" she'd asked.

"Yes. That is precisely what I mean."

"Oh." As relief had swept through her like a wave crashing up against the shore, Eleanor had hugged her arms to her chest and fought the urge to grin ear to ear. "That sounds splendid."

And live apart they had, for eleven months, three days, and…twenty-one minutes.

"You're really not going to try and guess?" Georgiana said with a sigh. "Fine. I'll tell you, but only because I cannot keep it to myself for a second longer." She smoothed an invisible wrinkle on her black skirt, hazel eyes demurely lowering to her lap before they suddenly lifted and pierced Eleanor with a smirking stare that filled her with immediate dread. "I've just received word from London…"

What remained of Eleanor's scone slid greasily down her throat as her entire spine stiffened. *Don't say it*, she thought silently. *Don't you dare say–*

"Derek is coming home!"

Chapter Six

"Don't leave." Her plump lips pursed in a persuasive pout, Vanessa stroked her hand down Derek's gleaming back – they'd just finished a *very* rigorous bout of lovemaking that had left them both perspiring and slightly breathless – before rolling onto her back, pink nipples pointing proudly up at the ceiling.

She could have easily reached for the sheet that was twisted around her hips and covered herself, but Vanessa was not a woman predisposed to modesty. It was one of the things Derek liked best about her. And one of the things he was going to miss the most when he traveled to Hawkridge Castle to tame his feral bride.

Standing, he splashed lukewarm water on his face before pulling on a pair of dove gray trousers and a white linen shirt. Buttoning his shirt he turned to face his mistress, his gaze leisurely traveling down her voluptuous figure before returning, with great reluctance, to her narrowed eyes. He knew she was displeased with him. Just like he knew there wasn't a damn thing he could do about it. Did she think he *wanted* to go chasing after Eleanor? Bloody hell, he'd rather gouge his eyes out with a dull spoon than tangle with that shrew again.

But his cousin had left him no choice.

Somehow, Lord Norton Bertram, the Earl of Glengarry, next in line to inherit the dukedom, and general pain in Derek's arse, had discovered the terms of their late grandfather's will. Mostly importantly the clause where Derek would be forced to forfeit the dukedom if he was not legally married before his twenty-ninth birthday.

In England, an unconsummated marriage could be grounds for annulment. It was no longer as common a practice as it once had been, but neither was it completely unheard of. Which meant Norton's daring threat to take him to court and seize the title for his own wasn't completely without merit.

The sniveling little wanker had actually had the audacity to stand in the middle of his study and demand *proof* that Derek had bedded his wife. As if it were the dark ages and the blood-stained sheet was being kept in a closet somewhere.

It had taken considerable self-restraint not to forcibly remove the smug look from Norton's face with his fist, but somehow he'd managed to show his cousin out without resorting to physical violence. Then he had immediately gone to his solicitor's office, who had told him, after a bit of hemming and hawing, that Norton *might* have a legitimate claim to the dukedom if their grandfather's will was brought into question in the court of appeals. After all, it was common knowledge that Derek and his duchess had been living completely apart for the better part of a year.

"There's no guarantee either way, of course," Mr. Banks had said anxiously. "But it would tie up the estate for months if not years, something which I believe you were hoping to avoid by marrying Lady Eleanor."

His solicitor was right. The predicament he now found himself in was *precisely* what he'd been trying to avoid when he'd married Eleanor. There was a part of him that knew he couldn't ignore her forever, of course. At some point he would need to produce a legitimate heir, if only to keep Norton's grasping hands off of *his* bloody title should he expire unexpectedly.

It wasn't so much the title itself that he cared about, or even the wealth. It was the knowledge that Norton and his wastrel ways would destroy everything their ancestors had so painstakingly built and preserved. The man was a charlatan and a gambler who had burned through his considerable inheritance in less than two years and was desperately looking for another way to refill his coffers. Well, Derek would be damned before he gave him the means to do so. Even if it meant returning to Hawkridge and wooing the last woman in all of England he wanted to look at, least of all bed.

His wife.

"I won't be gone for very long. Two fortnights at the most," he told Vanessa, reaching for a silky blonde curl. She batted his hand away.

"You're going to *her*," she spat, and Derek was surprised to see a stirring of jealousy in the depths of her frigid blue eyes. Vanessa may have been a passionate creature in bed, but out of it he'd never met another woman more detached or unfeeling which was what made her such an excellent mistress. He never had to worry about her doing something ridiculous, like falling in love with him. And while he knew she hadn't been pleased when he'd married Eleanor, she'd never said anything.

"Not because I want to." The overstuffed mattress creaked as he sat down beside her and traced his finger down one creamy thigh. This time she allowed him to touch her, but if she were a cat her tail would have been swishing back and forth in silent warning. "You knew I would have to do this at some point or another. It does not change anything between us."

"Doesn't it?" she asked, tilting her head.

"No. When I return we can pick up right…where…we…left…off." He punctuated each word with a kiss, working his way up her thigh to her breasts. Drawing a nipple between his lips he expertly swirled his tongue around the hard little bud, but when he felt her stiff and unyielding beneath him he sat back with a sigh. "You're making more of this than there has to be. It's not as if I am bringing the chit back to town with me."

"But you could," Vanessa pointed out, one pale brow arching. "If you so desired. She is your wife, after all."

"And you're my mistress." He raked a hand through his hair and stood up to prowl along the foot of the bed as he felt his patience beginning to wear thin. Their conversation was teetering dangerously close to a place neither one of them wished it to go. What did Vanessa want from him? To ignore his wife completely and let Norton steal the dukedom out from under his bloody nose?

He was going to Hawkridge for one reason and one reason only: to consummate his damn marriage. And once it was done, he would return to London and resume his life as if he'd never left.

"Let us also not forget *you're* married as well," he said, levelling a bland stare at Vanessa that bordered on annoyance. Arguing with his mistress was the last thing he wanted to do before travelling thirty miles to argue with his wife.

"That's different. My husband is a shriveled old man whose cock hasn't moved in eight years." The corners of her mouth tightened. "Your wife is young and beautiful."

Derek thought of Eleanor's shocking red hair and freckled cheeks and bit back a snort. "She's many things. Rude. Impertinent. Clumsy. But beautiful isn't one of them. You've nothing to be jealous of, Vanessa."

It was the wrong thing to say. He knew it even before her eyes flashed and her lips twisted in an elegant sneer.

"Of course I have nothing to be jealous of," she said coolly. "Eleanor is a country bumpkin who isn't fit to groom my horse, let alone be a duchess. You were a fool to ever marry her when there were a hundred other girls who would have been more suitable."

For the first time since their affair had begun nearly seven months ago, Derek felt a stirring of anger towards Vanessa. He didn't know where it stemmed from or what had caused it, only that he didn't care for his mistress making degrading comments about his wife. God knew that Eleanor had been an unusual choice, and Vanessa wasn't the only one who thought so. But his freckle-faced bride was *his* choice, for better or worse, and he wouldn't apologize for it or make excuses.

"Careful," he warned. "You are coming perilously close to overstepping your bounds"

"My *bounds*?" With a careless, tittering laugh Vanessa sat up and drew one long, silky leg to her chest. "I don't have bounds, Derek. And if you leave, you will no longer have a mistress."

"Are you giving me an ultimatum?" he said incredulously.

"Call it whatever you wish."

His jaw tightened. He'd truly thought he and Vanessa would have more time…but if there was one rule he followed without fail, it was to always end an affair before it became personal.

Unlike other men, Derek did not have affairs because he was lonely or wanted companionship. When he took a mistress, it was because he was after one thing: unadulterated pleasure. And when that mistress could no longer give him what he desired, he settled a large sum on her and went on his way without remorse or regret.

"My solicitor will see that you are taken care of," he said curtly before he picked up his waistcoat and left the room without so much as a backwards glance.

It was a cold, emotionless end to a scandalously hot affair that had lasted for more than seven months. But if there was one lesson he'd learned from his parents and their untimely demise, it was that it was always better to be the one leaving than the one who was left.

Mistresses were easily replaced, especially when there were no attachments formed. And he always took great pains to make sure there never were. It wasn't that he didn't believe in love. It was simply that he didn't believe in love for *himself*. He never had, and despite his countless affairs – or mayhap because of them – he doubted if he ever would.

Love was for poets and dreamers, not for cynical dukes.

And certainly not for a cynical duke with a wife who kept a hedgehog in her pocket.

Chapter Seven

Rain fell relentlessly from a gray and cloudy sky. It was the third spring shower in as many days, which was why Eleanor knew – or at least hoped – it would soon clear. Having gone out early in the morning to care for her animals, she was now stuck inside the carriage shed until the rain lifted.

The sweet smell of hay permeated the air, while the soft ruffle of feathers and gentle squeaks and snorts (just yesterday she'd rescued two run piglets from a sow who wanted nothing to do with them) created a lilting symphony of contended sounds. If not for her grumbling stomach – and the veritable feast of eggs and bread and sausage that awaited her inside – she would have been perfectly happy to remain in the carriage shed for half the day, if not longer. Especially since any hour (any minute, really) a formidable black coach was going to come trotting up the drive and a man she very much did not want to see was going to emerge.

Her stomach as she imagined seeing her husband again. Husband. How strange it felt to even *think* that word! Oh, why did the duke have to come to Hawkridge? She knew it wasn't to see her. He'd made it very clear when he had banished her to the country that he had absolutely no interest in her whatsoever. What was it he had growled at her as he'd all but shoved her into the carriage after the church ceremony was over? Ah yes, now she remembered.

"I hope you enjoy Surrey. You're going to be there for a very long time."

Such a romantic, her husband. Sitting cross-legged in a pile of straw, Eleanor reached behind her to draw the piglet she'd dubbed Sir Galahad into her lap. He wiggled when she scratched behind one floppy ear, his tiny wet nostrils quivering with delight, before promptly sprawling his pink body across her leg and falling asleep. Eleanor sighed. Sir Galahad had more manners and decorum in one little pork chop than the Duke of Hawkridge had in his entire body. She liked to think time had improved her husband's demeanor, but she sincerely doubted it. In her experience men were who they were, and pampered, titled men were the worst of the lot. If only Henny hadn't stolen her hair pin...but there was no use crying over spilt milk.

"Look Sir Galahad," she murmured, glancing up at

the window. "The rain has slowed." Carefully moving the sleeping piglet off her lap, she tip-toed through the straw and slipped out of the carriage shed before any of her pets were the wiser.

She'd already set the bar in place over the door when she realized she'd forgotten her gloves and hat inside. Gnawing on her bottom lip she considered dashing back in to retrieve them, but that would only cause a ruckus and besides, it was hardly raining at all. No more than a mist, really.

A mist that abruptly turned into a downpour when she was less than halfway to the manor.

With a loud shriek Eleanor pulled up her dress, kicked off her flimsy shoes, and raced barefoot across the lawn. She was in such a hurry to get inside that she failed to notice the stately coach pulled by a matching team of bays sitting at the end of the drive. But when she skidded haphazardly into the foyer there was no avoiding the hard chest that greeted her, nor the man the hard chest belonged to.

Her yelp of surprise was swallowed up by a black greatcoat that smelled faintly of cigar smoke. Strong hands closed around her wrists, trapping them in a manacle like grip. Eleanor found herself tilting her head back and looking up, up, up into a strikingly handsome countenance with bold lips pulled back in a frown, freshly shaven jaw clenched tight, and brandy colored eyes flashing with annoyance. She blinked, and water spilled from her lashes to run down her cheeks in delicate rivulets as a tentative smile curved her mouth.

"I'm sorry," she said contritely, wanting to at least *try* to get off on the right foot this time. Who knew, maybe her husband really *had* changed, in which case it was only fair to give him the benefit of the doubt. "I was in a rush and didn't see you standing there."

"Clearly," Derek drawled, his insufferable tone and cold sneer instantly confirming all of her worst fears. The duke wasn't any kinder or less arrogant than he'd been a year ago. If anything, he was *worse*! Her smile dimming, she tried to pull her hands free, but his grip – while painless – was unrelenting.

"Let me get a good look at you," he said, and her eyes narrowed to thin slits of enraged emerald when he began a slow, thorough examination of her body as if she were a horse standing at market.

"Are you quite finished?" she demanded when his gaze returned at last to her face.

"Quite. I must say, when I sent word of my arrival I had hoped to be greeted by the Duchess of Hawkridge, not a drowned rat that vaguely resembles the woman I married." Releasing her wrists, he took a step back and scowled down at her, dark brows forming a rigid line of disapproval above eyes that had deepened to a rich shade of brown. "Where is your hat? Your gloves? Your cloak? And what the devil were you doing outside to begin with? It's bloody well pouring."

"Is it?" Eleanor said with a feigned gasp. "My goodness, I hadn't noticed. That must be why I'm all wet."

"I see time hasn't dulled your sarcastic wit."

"Nor has it cured you of your arrogance," she retorted.

They stared hard at one another, neither one willing to be the first to look away. Trapped in a battle of silent wills, they might have stood there all day were it not for Georgiana's sudden arrival.

"Derek! You're here at last!" The dark haired beauty swept across the foyer with enviable grace. Stepping between husband and wife, she subtly nudged Eleanor out of the way before draping her arms around her brother's shoulders and pressing a quick kiss to his cheek. "How exhausted you must be after such a long and arduous journey."

"He only came from London," Eleanor couldn't help but point out. "It's not as if he just sailed across the Atlantic."

"Maybe not, but it appears as though you have." Georgiana's nose wrinkled. "Why are you sopping wet? And what is that *smell*?"

"I don't smell anything," Eleanor said defensively even as she lifted a damp strand of hair and took a quick sniff. Aside from the faint smell of hay – a scent she found quite pleasant – she detected nothing odorous. But apparently she was the only one.

"My sister is correct," said Derek, stepping away. "There is a certain...aroma...emanating from your general direction. Please bathe and make yourself presentable before dinner."

Effectively dismissed, Eleanor was only too happy to make her escape. Walking quickly out of the foyer, she made a quick detour to the library where Henny was dozing on a pillow in front of the fire and carried the yawning hedgehog up to her private bedchamber. Then, because a late morning nap seemed like an absolutely splendid idea, she stripped down to her linen corset and drawers, settled Henny beside her on the bed, and, lulled by the gentle smattering of rain against the windows, promptly drifted off to sleep.

WELL THAT HADN'T gone as well as he'd hoped. Grinding his teeth together in frustration, Derek stalked into his study and slammed the door in his wake, a loud indication that he was not to be disturbed.

In anticipation of his arrival the large room, trimmed in mahogany and dark blue drapes, had been swept, dusted, and polished with beeswax. Not a small undertaking given the long wall of floor to ceiling bookshelves and heavy leather furniture, but his staff was nothing if not well trained. Unfortunately, the same could not be said of his wife.

He had hoped a year in the country with Georgiana might have civilized Eleanor, but if her mud-splattered dress and mop of wet hair were any indication she'd gotten *worse* instead of better. He had come to Hawkridge expecting to be greeted by a woman who at least resembled a duchess in appearance if not demeanor. Instead he'd gotten a wet street urchin who had looked as if she'd been dragged in off the streets of St Giles.

Sitting heavily behind his desk, he poured himself a glass of brandy and leaned back in his chair. He stared hard at the ceiling, studying a narrow crack in the white plaster as he wondered how the hell he was going to woo a wife that was more wild than tame.

Derek knew he would be well within his husbandly rights to force himself upon her, but his stomach rebelled at the thought. If their marriage was consummated – *when* it was consummated, he corrected as he sat up and took a sip of brandy – Eleanor would be a willing participant. He'd make sure of it. After all, underneath all that mud and behind that shrewish temper was a woman like any other. And if there was one thing he knew how to do, it was charm a woman.

She'll be eating out of my palm before the end of the week, he thought confidently before he finished the rest of his brandy and prowled to the large bay window overlooking the east lawn. If not for a heavy fog he would have had a clear view of the stables. Instead the only thing he could make out through the hazy gray mist was the bronze weathervane perched atop the largest barn. A fiftieth anniversary present from his grandmother to his grandfather, it was a large destrier in full gallop. Every year his grandfather had seen to it that the weathervane was taken down and polished, but since his death it had gone untouched and a faint patina had begun to set it, giving the stallion's mane and tail a greenish tint.

Absently drumming his fingers along the wooden sill, Derek turned around and let his head fall back against the cool glass with a dull *thud*. Five years he'd been the duke, and some days it still felt as though his grandfather was standing around the corner, just waiting to lay into him with a blustering diatribe about how much of a disappointment he was. No matter what he'd done, it had never been enough to earn the late duke's approval…or his respect.

The cantankerous old bastard had made it very clear he wished it was his son inheriting the title instead of his 'worthless wastrel of a grandson'. He'd snarled the words so many times that they'd become imprinted in Derek's subconscious, and more than once he could have sworn he had heard the raspy whisper of his grandfather's voice late at night when the halls were dark and the moon shone bright.

Hawkridge Castle may have been the pride and jewel of the dukedom and where he'd spent most of his childhood, but it would never be home. Not as long as his grandfather's memory continued to lurk in every shadow and corner.

Pushing away from the window, he returned to his desk and picked up a quill pen. If he was going to be stuck in this Godforsaken place for the undeterminable future, he might as well make the best of it. His solicitor usually took care of his business correspondences, but the man's wife was expecting a child any day so he had been unable to leave London which meant Derek was – at least temporarily – in charge of his own affairs. Having always had a good head for numbers and a fluid hand, he didn't mind the extra work. In fact, it was just the distraction he needed.

A distraction from ghosts.

A distraction from piqued mistresses.

And, most importantly, a distraction from red-haired wives with waspish tongues and the biggest, greenest eyes he'd ever seen…

Chapter Eight

Eleanor was just emerging from the tub after a long hot soak when the door to her bedchamber suddenly swung open and her husband stormed in. With a loud gasp she instinctively reached for the nearest thing to cover herself with. In this case, a sheer silk wrapper her maid had left draped over the bathing screen. Unfortunately, the flimsy material did little to conceal her nakedness. Instead it clung to her damp flesh like a second skin, and her entire face flushed a dull, deep red when she realized every inch of her body was on full display in the flickering candlelight, from her dusky pink nipples to the soft nest of auburn curls between her thighs.

"What are you *doing* in here?" she exclaimed. "Get out at once!"

For his part the duke seemed just as startled as she was and his eyes immediately fixed on a point somewhere above her left shoulder. "I – I was, um...That is to say I was, er...you're naked."

It was the first time she'd ever heard him stutter. Awkwardly draping one arm across her chest and flattening the other over her stomach, she crossed her legs and glared. "Thank you for pointing out the obvious! Now would you *please* leave?"

"Yes…ah…all right." But no sooner had he walked out of the room than he turned around and walked right back in. "Why weren't you at dinner?"

"I – what?" This time it was Eleanor who found herself at a loss for words.

"Dinner," he repeated. "You weren't there." His gaze dropped to her face then down to her breasts where it lingered for the span of a heartbeat before quickly returning to her pink countenance. A muscle ticked high in his right cheek. "I thought I made it very clear in the foyer that I wished for you to join me for dinner."

"I wasn't hungry."

"Regardless of whether you were hungry or not, when I give you a command I expect it to be followed," he said imperiously.

"A command?" Her eyebrows shot up. "You do not command me. I am your wife, not a dog."

Derek started to say something, but seemed to change his mind at the least second. Instead he lowered his head and, pinching the bridge of his nose, drew a deep breath. When he looked up again his expression was calm, but Eleanor still detected a hint of glittering temper in the depths of his gaze. "From now on, I should very much like if we dined together."

"Why?" she asked suspiciously. First he'd shown up out of the clear blue after nearly a year gone by without so much as a letter to inquire as to how she was faring, and now he wanted to dine with her? Her husband was clearly up to something.

"Why?" he repeated. "Because, as you yourself just said, you are my wife. I would like the opportunity to get to know you better." A smile lifted one side of his mouth. It was a very handsome smile. A very charming smile. The sort of smile a man might give to the woman he was courting in the hopes of winning her favor.

Definitely up to something, Eleanor decided.

"This wasn't a marriage either one of us planned," he continued. "But that does not mean we have to be enemies."

She shifted her weight as her foot began to tingle. "I don't think of us as enemies."

"But do you think of us as friends? I thought not," he said when she pressed her lips together. "I'd like us to start over, if we could. Forget the circumstances that brought us here, and go forward with a fresh slate. I'm extending an olive branch, Eleanor. And I would like very much if you'd take it."

She had never been very fond of olives. Too bitter for her taste. But if Derek really *was* making a genuine effort to improve their tumultuous relationship, then she could try to do the same. After all, it wasn't as if she enjoyed fighting with him. Well, at least not all the time.

"Very well," she said, giving the tiniest of nods.

"Excellent." He started to walk towards her, but at her wary frown he stopped short and lifted an innocent brow. "What? A man cannot kiss his wife goodnight?"

Her grip on the wrap tightened. "I thought you just wanted to have dinner together. You did not say anything about kissing."

"We *are* married," he reasoned. "I thought it was a forgone conclusion that we would kiss at some point." Even white teeth flashed in a grin that could only be described as roguish. He raked a hand through his hair, drawing her gaze to his thick ebony locks. Almost absently she wondered what the silky tresses would feel like. Coarse, like the mane of a horse? Or smooth, like the downy fur of a rabbit?

"I suppose one *small* kiss wouldn't hurt anything," she said reluctantly. "We have to start somewhere, don't we?"

"That we do."

She tensed when he crossed the room in three long, languid strides, but to her pleasant surprise his touch was surprisingly gentle when he wrapped his hand around the nape of her neck, his fingers tangling in the damp tendrils that had come undone from the twisted pile of curls atop her head.

"Relax," he said softly, his thumb gently massaging a knotted cord of muscle. He was standing so close she could smell the faintest hint of wine of his breath. Madeira, if she had to hazard a guess. A sweet red wine that went splendidly with dessert and the only spirit her mother had allowed her to drink at the dinner table. "There's no reason to be frightened."

"I'm n-not frightened." It was a lie. If she'd been wearing boots she would have been quaking in them. It wasn't that she was scared of Derek, per say. He may have been an arrogant cad prone to flashes of temper, but he wasn't violent. She knew he wouldn't hurt her, or force himself upon her. So why were her knees trembling? And why did her belly feel as though she was in a coach that had just taken a very sharp turn downhill?

The kissing, she decided. It had to be the kissing. Having never done it before, she didn't have the slightest idea what to expect. Was she supposed to close her eyes? What did she do with her hands? Should she purse her lips like a fish, or pinch them closed? For a woman who was accustomed to being knowledgeable on a vast array of subjects, from Greek mythology to astronomy and everything in between, the idea of *not* knowing how something worked was incredibly daunting.

"I – I've changed my mind," she said nervously. "I don't think–"

But it was too late. The hand at the back of her neck tightened ever-so-slightly as Derek lowered his head and kissed her. His mouth was warm and dry. She could taste the wine on his lips – she'd been right, it *was* Madeira – and she couldn't help but wonder if he tasted what she'd had for dinner. It wasn't the most romantic thought, but then no one had ever accused Eleanor of being a romantic. An academic, yes. A bluestocking, certainly. But a romantic? No. Never that.

Yet she couldn't help but feel a bit of romance blossoming within her as Derek deepened the kiss. His eyes were closed so she closed hers as well, and when he wrapped his arm around the small of her back and drew her against the hard length of his body she tentatively splayed her hands across his chest.

She felt more than heard his sharp intake of breath at her innocent touch, and she marveled that such a small motion could cause such a large reaction. Then she felt his tongue lightly slide across the seam of her lips and it was her turn to gasp, for surely this was *not* how kissing was done.

"It's all right," he murmured huskily. "I just want to taste you. Just a taste…"

Her stomach fluttered at his words and after a

moment's hesitation she parted her lips, welcoming his tongue into her mouth on a soft, wondering sigh.

Oh yes, she thought dazedly. *This* is *how kissing is done*.

To her embarrassment – and secret delight – she felt her nipples harden against his chest. If his low growl of approval was any indication he'd felt them as well, and she was glad they'd both decided to close their eyes so he couldn't see the bright pink blush unraveling across her cheeks. The blush traveled all the way down to her collarbones when, without so much as an, *'I'm going to kiss your ear now and you'd best prepare yourself for it's going to set your blood on fire'* he did precisely that.

Her eyes shot open as his teeth scraped against her earlobe. She clung to him, latching onto his waistcoat for dear life as her legs threatened to give out. When he teased his tongue along the delicate shell of her ear she *would* have collapsed if not for the arm he had wrapped around her back. He held her upright, which was a very good thing for she felt as if her entire body had suddenly turned to a bowl of orange jelly. Goodness! All these years she'd thought her ears were only for hearing. If she'd known the truth, she might have been tempted to investigate this kissing business *much* earlier.

Derek's mouth slid down to her neck where it pressed against her fluttering pulse before returning to her lips. A few more slow, leisurely thrusts of his tongue and then, to Eleanor's great disappointment, it was all over.

"That's it?" she asked, her forehead creasing in a frown.

"No." Brandy eyes dark and heavy, Derek tucked a loose tendril of hair behind her ear before he stepped back. "That wasn't even a scratch on the surface, Red."

"Then why did you stop?" And why was she filled with a vague ache, as if she'd left something undone? The feeling was an uncomfortable one, and with a grimace she tried to ease it by pressing her thighs together. Seeing the tiny, nearly imperceptible movement her husband's gaze grew hot, but he didn't kiss her again. Instead he took another step back, and then another until he was standing in front of the door

"Because I can't trust myself." His tone was almost accusatory, as if he was blaming *her* for…well, come to think of it she hadn't the vaguest idea. Had she done something wrong? She knew she wasn't an expert kisser by any means – how could she be, having never done it before? – but he hadn't seemed displeased.

She bit her bottom lip, drawing the swollen flesh between her teeth to worry it back and forth as a dog might a bone. For some reason that seemed to make Derek even angrier, for with a sharp curse he abruptly turned on his heel and stalked out of the room, leaving her staring after him in complete bewilderment.

Chapter Nine

What the devil had just happened?

Massaging his temples where a dull throbbing had settled in – while simultaneously trying to ignore the *other* dull throbbing between his legs – Derek entered the library and threw himself down into a chair to stare broodingly at the smoldering fire.

With the exception of his own thoughts and the crackle and hiss of the flames, the house was quiet, the servants having long ago found their beds. They would be up before the sun rose to attend the hearths, open the drapes, make breakfast. Under their care – and the sharp eye of Mrs. Gibbons – Hawkridge Castle ran like a well-oiled machine, which was precisely how he liked it. When he woke in the morning there were never any surprises. He always knew just what to expect.

He knew there would be a warm basin of water already filled so he could shave his face (he preferred to do it himself rather than relying on a personal valet). He knew as soon as he came downstairs a piping hot cup of coffee, two poached eggs, and the newest edition of The Morning Post would be awaiting him in the solarium. He knew his riding clothes would be laid out on the bed when he returned upstairs to dress, and he knew his horse would be waiting for him, already tacked, in front of the stables.

His house in London ran in a similar fashion. Having started his life in one direction only to have it veer dramatically off course when his parents died, he was a man who enjoyed order. Who liked knowing what was going to come next. Who did not care for surprises. Which was why his little red-haired wife, with her sharp tongue and quick wit and guileless green eyes a man could lose himself in if he wasn't careful, had thrown him so utterly and completely off guard.

Consummate the marriage and get the hell out of this Godforsaken castle where painful memories were as plentiful as rocks. *That* was his plan. Or at least, that had been his plan before he'd kissed her.

Eleanor was an inconvenience. A means to an end. A way for him to continue his neat, orderly life while still meeting the terms of the will. So why had he just been one second removed from losing all self-control, throwing his virgin wife onto the bed, and rutting into her like a savage?

He knew what lust felt like. He was more than well acquainted with passion. But what he'd just experienced upstairs…it was unlike anything he'd ever known. It had been more than lust. More than passion.

One glancing kiss. That was all he had intended. But from the first moment he first tasted the sweet honey of her lips he'd wanted more. He'd *craved* more. And he didn't know why.

Eleanor was by no means experienced. He wouldn't have been the least bit surprised to learn that was her very first kiss. Yet despite her innocence, she'd entranced him like no other woman before her. Bracing his elbows on his knees, he leaned forward and buried his head in his hands. It just didn't make any bloody *sense*. This wasn't supposed to happen. He wasn't supposed to desire his own wife.

No, not desire, he corrected himself grimly. Desire was too weak of a word. Yearning came close, but it was still insufficient. There was no word in the English language to describe what he'd felt. The power of it. The thrall. The ache. All of his mistresses combined had never made him feel even an ounce of whatever the hell it was he'd felt with Eleanor. And that was the bloody point. He didn't *want* to feel. Feeling led to emotions, emotions led to disorder, disorder led to chaos.

Sitting back, he cupped the nape of his neck and directed his brooding stare back into the flames. All this, he thought with a bitter twist of his lips, and all he'd done was kiss her. What the devil would happen when he actually bedded her?

"Derek? Are you in here?" Georgiana's lilting voice pierced the silence, followed by the rhythmic swish of her skirts as she strolled into the library and discovered him sitting in front of the fire. "Sitting by yourself in the dark without a glass of brandy?" She made a *tsking* sound under her breath. "It must be serious. Care if I join you?"

"Go ahead." He nodded brusquely at the empty chair beside him. She sat down, and for a moment the two siblings gazed at the slowly burning logs without speaking.

Their relationship had always been, if not troubled, then at the very least strained. With only two years separating them they'd been thick as thieves when they were children. More than once person confused them for twins they were so close, and one never did something without the other. Then their parents died...and everything changed.

Georgiana was immediately taken under their grandmother's wing, but it was their grandfather who sent her away to boarding school. She hadn't wanted to go. Had begged Derek to help her stay. But as a boy of only twelve there'd been nothing he could do but watch through a sheen of angry tears as her carriage drove further and further away.

When she returned four years later she was a

different person. Or at least that was how it seemed to Derek. Gone was the rebellious tomboy who had loved to climb trees and catch frogs. In her place was a quiet, polite, ladylike stranger who no longer looked at him as if he'd hung the moon. In fact, she'd been so busy preparing for her formal debut she'd hardly looked at him at all. Over the next two years they grew even further apart, and when she married her count he felt as if he were attending the wedding of a stranger.

This was the first time they'd been under the same roof in nearly a decade. She was his closest living relative – he didn't count Norton – and he didn't know what to say to her. Shifting his weight, he cast a surreptitious glance at her profile out of the corner of his eye.

"You're up late," he noted.

"I often have trouble falling asleep," she said without looking away from the fire. "I find it helps to read."

Which must have been why she'd come into the library. "I can leave."

"No, stay. Please," she added when he started to stand. "Do you know this is the first time we've lived in the same house since I married James?"

Derek nodded. "I just had the same thought."

"I miss him the most at night. It must be the quiet, for I hardly think of him at all during the day. Do you think that's strange?"

"No," he said, for he often found himself thinking of their parents in a similar fashion. "I don't think it's strange at all. It has only been seven months, Georgiana."

The ghost of a smile touched her lips. "Seven months..." she murmured. "Sometimes it feels like a lifetime. Other days I expect to turn my head and see him still standing behind me."

He didn't know what to say to that, so he said nothing.

"I didn't love him," she continued after a long pause. "But I did like him. He was kind, if a bit boring. We were trying to have a child when he passed. For a while I hoped...but it wasn't meant to be, I suppose. Just as well. Children are messy creatures. Always getting into this and that. When do you think you and Eleanor will have them?"

Startling slightly at the sound of his wife's name, he crossed his arms and frowned at the fire. It was nearly out, having smoldered down to a few logs that glowed orange and red in the dark. "I don't know. Eventually, I suppose. I need an heir."

"Yes, you do. Unless you want to tie Hawkridge up in a pretty red bow and hand it over to Norton."

"I am well aware."

"Then what are you doing down here instead of upstairs with your wife you haven't seen in nearly a year?" One elegant black brow arched as she finally turned her head to look at him. "A wife whom, if I remember correctly, you sent on her merry way as soon as the marriage ceremony was concluded. You didn't even let the poor thing partake in her wedding feast and she so does *love* to eat."

"I thought she would be happier in the country." The feeble excuse was the same he'd used when anyone else had inquired as to Eleanor's whereabouts in the months following their wedding. Poor health, he'd said. She does best in the fresh air. No one believed him, of course. Wives – especially new ones – were never *really* sent to the country for their health. But it was what a husband was expected to say even when the truth was painfully obvious.

"Eleanor is the healthiest person I've ever met," said Georgiana, her lifted brow indicating she didn't believe him for a moment. "Surprising, really, given all the time she spends with those animals of hers."

"Animals?" He knew his wife had a hedgehog named Penny or Whinny. Ginny, maybe? He'd considered forbidding her to bring the pet to Hawkridge – God knew the spiky little rat had already caused enough trouble – but he hadn't wanted the headache of another long, drawn out argument.

"Yes. She has an entire barn full of them. Geese and pigs and rodents and heaven knows what else."

Georgiana flicked her wrist. "All rescued or saved in some manner or another. She's a regular animal Joan of Arc, your Eleanor."

"She isn't *my* Eleanor," he scowled.

"Oh?" his sister said with a hint of amusement. "Then just whom does she belong to?"

No one, was his immediate thought. *Eleanor belongs to no one.* She was like a wild filly who'd not yet been tamed. One that had never felt the constrictive binding of a halter or the cold metal of a bit pressed between its teeth. After their kiss, he'd be lying if he said he wasn't looking forward to gentling her.

"I like her, you know," Georgiana said when he remained silent. "Although she *is* an unconventional choice for a duchess. She would have been much better suited if she married a baron, I think. Or mayhap a doctor."

Derek straightened in his chair. "Are you saying I'm not suitable enough for her?"

"No. I am simply saying she is not who I would have picked for your wife. But the damage has been done, as they say, and there's no going back now." She propped up her chin on the palm of her hand and blinked languidly at him. "What do you plan to do with her?"

"*Do* with her? She isn't a piece of furniture to be polished and packed away."

"And yet that is precisely what you've done. Married

her and packed her away. Which makes me wonder what you're doing here now."

His scowl deepened. "I thought you were happy to see me."

"I was. I am. Now that James has passed, you and Eleanor are the only family I have."

"What about Norton?" he asked, wanting to gauge his sister's attachment to their slimy weasel of a cousin. If the will was brought to court, Georgiana could prove to be a useful ally. Her husband's family had high connections, including a magistrate. He had been waiting to tell her about their grandfather's will until he knew for certain where her allegiances lay.

"I'd rather be related to one of your wife's pigs," she said with a sniff. "I claim no relation to that wastrel."

"Good. In that case, I have something to tell you..."

"Grandfather always did like to have the last word, didn't he?" Georgiana said once Derek had finished.

"Grandfather was a tyrannical bastard who wished I had died instead of Father," Derek said flatly.

"I won't argue with you." She sat back, her fingers pressing together as she gazed contemplatively into the fire. "So that's why you've returned. To save the dukedom by sleeping with your own wife. How very noble of you."

When she put it that way...

"I would have gotten around to consummating the

marriage eventually," he said.

"What's stopping you now?" his sister demanded. "I assume you want this matter over and done with as quickly as possible so you can return to your life in London. I was a married woman, and as such I know that the deed cannot be done with you down here and her up there."

"In case you haven't noticed, Eleanor is not exactly fond of me." He glanced at the fire. Save one log that stubbornly refused to yield to the flames, it had all but gone out.

"And?" Georgiana challenged. "You're the Duke of Hawkridge. Your reputation proceeds you wherever you go. They say there isn't a woman you cannot woo into your bed with no more than a look. So woo you wife, meet the terms of the will, and be done with it. Let's not forget the woman carries a *hedgehog* with her wherever she goes. How hard could it possibly be?"

Chapter Ten

How hard was it to charm a woman who kept a hedgehog in her pocket? Very hard, as soon Derek discovered for himself over the next five days. Very hard indeed. Especially since Eleanor seemed to be going out of her way to avoid him.

When he ventured outside she snuck back in. When he went in search of her inside the house she slipped back out. The only time he saw her for more than a few minutes was when they dined together, but even then she proved to be completely immune to his attempts at seduction.

He stroked his hand down her arm and she brushed it away as if it were a bothersome gnat. He pulled out her chair before she sat down and she informed in no uncertain terms that she was perfectly capable of pulling out her own chair, thank you very much, and she didn't need a man to do it for her. She'd fed the bouquet of flowers he picked for her to the goat. When he asked if she wanted to go on a moonlit walk around the pond she said she was too tired, and then two hours later he glanced out the window and caught her scampering around the lawn in the dark catching fireflies.

Which was why he was so surprised when she barged into his office in the middle of the afternoon and demanded his immediate assistance in a matter of life or death…

SPRING WAS A busy time for animals, which meant it was a busy time for Eleanor. She'd found not one, not two, but *three* different nests that had become dislodged from their perch after a rainstorm. They were all filled to the brim with chirping baby birds, and after trying – and failing – to return them to the trees they'd tumbled out of, she'd resorted to caring for the babies herself. Not an easy task, given they had to fed worms every few hours.

And she had to dig the worms up herself.

But she didn't mind the work. She didn't even mind the dirt. What she *did* mind was Derek following her around like a little lost puppy wherever she went. The man was making a damned nuisance of himself. It seemed as if every time she turned around there he was with a flowery compliment (*'you're looking simply ravishing this evening'* and *'your hair is the color of a fiery sunset* were two of his favorites, even though she *knew* he abhorred her red hair) or a handful of roses or a shiny piece of jewelry. The worst of it was when he pretended she was an invalid and insisted on pulling out every single chair she tried to sit down in, or rushed to escort her up the stairs, or – in one particularly memorable case – whisked off his jacket and placed it on the ground so she wouldn't have to step in a teensy tiny puddle of mud. Truth be told she hadn't minded the last (it had been strangely satisfying to grind her heel into his fancy satin-lined coat), but the first two weren't to be borne.

It wasn't that she *disliked* the attention. He was, after all, her husband. But she absolutely hated that it all seemed so rehearsed, like a play that kept running over and over again even though it was poorly acted and the sets were in complete disrepair.

What she wouldn't have given for a dash of spontaneity! Like the night he'd appeared in her bedchamber and kissed her positively senseless. That certainly hadn't been rehearsed. To her disappointment, however, he'd kept his lips to himself...and even though she'd considered kissing *him*, she hadn't quite yet managed to gather the courage.

"It's quite a predicament, isn't it Henny?" she asked her hedgehog as they strolled leisurely around the pond. Henny waddled cheerfully besides her, stopping every so often to sniff out a grub in the bright green grass.

It was a beautiful spring afternoon, the sky a clear,

endless blue with nary a cloud in sight. She tipped her head back and closed her eyes, enjoying the warmth of the sun after two gray, gloomy days of rain. Birds sang from the treetops as they busily flitted from branch to branch, their beaks filled with tufts of horse hair and pieces of straw. From one of the pastures came the distant echo of hooves as the young foals frolicked next to their dams, and a cow's chiding moo as it called out to a calf that had wandered too far. It was a time of renewal and rebirth, of hope and wonder, of confusion and speculation.

"If only I knew what he *wanted*," Eleanor mused as she opened her eyes and resumed walking. "What do you think, Henny?"

But if the hedgehog knew why the duke had suddenly turned from a mocking, arrogant scoundrel into a sweet, doting husband, she kept it to herself.

They rounded the far edge of the pond and started back towards the house. Eleanor slowed her steps to keep pace with Henny's considerably shorter legs, and even though she was tempted to scoop the hedgehog into her pocket, she knew her beloved pet needed the exercise after a long winter with too little activity and too many crumpets.

Belatedly remembering to put on her hat before they came into view of the manor, she tugged the bothersome bonnet down over her head and was just beginning to tie the strings when the frantic sound of honking filled the air.

"Oh no," she breathed when the honking was swiftly followed by Mrs. Gibbons' blustering shout and the unmistakable *thwack* of something very sharp striking something very hard. "The geese must have gotten out again! Henny, come on. We have to hurry!"

Picking her pet up by her soft underbelly, she dropped the wiggling hedgehog into the pocket of her cornflower blue dress, picked up her skirts, and raced towards the house as fast as her legs would carry her.

She'd just reached the outside door to the kitchen when it flew open and poor Donald, his white wings extended and neck stretched out in alarm, came flapping out followed closely by Mrs. Gibbons yielding a large butcher's knife.

"I'll get you this time you damned rascal," the housekeeper said grimly. "You'll not evade the pot again!"

"Mrs. Gibbons, what are you doing?" Eleanor cried. "Put that knife down at once! You're going to hurt someone!'"

"Aye," the housekeeper said grimly. "I'm going hurt this goose! I warned you, Your Grace. If that feathered fiend ever dared enter my household again he would be tossed straight in the stew!" With that dire threat she chased Donald around the corner and out of sight.

Realizing the housekeeper wasn't going to listen to her, Eleanor dashed into the house and ran straight to her husband's study. She barged in without knocking, her frantic gaze seeking and immediately finding Derek sitting behind his desk. He half rose when he saw her, dark brow furrowing.

"Eleanor? What–"

"You have to come at once! Mrs. Gibbons is trying to murder Donald!"

His eyes widened. "Mrs. Gibbons is trying to murder the new footman?"

"No!" Grabbing his arm when he came around his desk, she half pulled, half dragged him out of the study. "Donald the goose!"

"I don't understand–"

"This is no time to argue!" Eleanor yelped. "It's a matter of life and death!"

They caused quite the spectacle as they ran through the kitchens. The duchess, her cheeks flushed and her bonnet askew, with the duke right on her heels and a hedgehog clinging for dear life to the edge of the duchess's pocket. Maids dropped whatever they were doing in their haste to jump out of the way, including a large bowl of flour that hit the table with a clatter and sent a cloud of white flying up into the air.

Following the sounds of Mrs. Gibbons' shouts and Donald's desperate honking, Eleanor discovered the enraged housekeeper and the terrified goose behind the stone greenhouse. Mrs. Gibbons had managed to pin Donald in a corner and the goose was alternating between hissing and honking, snapping his beak whenever the housekeeper tried to strike him with the butcher's knife.

"*Do* something," Eleanor told her husband desperately.

Only later would she realize it was the first time she had ever asked for his help. And much, much later she would look back at the memory and smile, for – even though she didn't know it then – it marked a momentous turning point in their relationship. But of course she didn't think of any of that *now*. How could she, with Donald's life hanging in the balance?

"Please," she whispered, gazing up at Derek imploringly.

He lifted his hand and brushed his thumb across her cheek. It was a glancing touch, but no less powerful for its brevity. Eleanor felt a shiver of awareness ripple down her spine when their eyes met, worried green sinking into steady golden brown. There was a dusting of white flour on his nose and chin, but in that moment – at least to her – he'd never looked more like a duke.

"Don't worry," he said quietly before he turned and marched up to Mrs. Gibbons.

Helpless to do anything but watch and wait, Eleanor

clasped her hands together as he and the housekeeper had a terse exchange. She couldn't hear what was being said over Donald's honking, but whatever it was caused Mrs. Gibbons face to drain of all color and the knife to drop from her hand. Eleanor breathed a heavy sigh of relief when the sharp blade sank harmlessly into the ground. Sensing the danger had passed, Donald immediately stopped honking and, with one last hiss at his arch nemesis, ran straight to Eleanor who crouched down and wrapped her arms around his trembling body.

"You stupid goose," she said with great affection. "Why couldn't you have just stayed put? Go on, then. Back to the carriage barn with you."

Donald lovingly rubbed his head against her knee. Sitting back on her heels, Eleanor watched him waddle away with a faint smile curving her lips. She was going to miss Donald and Ronald when she released them into the pond, but she knew they would be happier there than cooped up in a barn. As soon as their house was finished – a floating apparatus she'd designed herself that would be anchored to the middle of the pond and keep them safe from a prowling fox – they'd be ready to make the transition. She would still visit them every day, and–

"*Ahem.*"

She turned at the masculine sound of a throat being cleared, and found herself staring at a pair of mud splattered hessians. Tilting her head back, her gaze traveled up across a pair of powerful thighs encased in gray breeches, over a flat abdomen that led to a broad, muscular chest, and finally stopped on her husband's flour covered face.

Looking down at her with an expression that teetered between amusement and exasperation, he held out his hand. "Sir Donald has officially been pardoned for all crimes against the crown," he said formally, and Eleanor felt the corners of her mouth twitch.

"I should like it put on the official record that he was never actually found guilty of any of those crimes. He was the victim of wrongful persecution."

"On what grounds?" the duke asked, lifting a brow.

"On the grounds of his being a goose of course," she said, as if it were obvious, and now Derek was the one who smiled.

It was a very nice smile. The kind that was neither forced nor practiced, and crinkled the corners of his eyes. Feeling the same flutter in her belly as she had right before he kissed her, Eleanor hesitantly placed her small hand in his larger one and allowed him to lift her to her feet. She waited for him to let her go. To make some snide remark about her appearance. Instead his grip tightened. Their fingers interlocking, he pulled her slowly towards him as their smiles faded away.

"You have flour in your hair," he said, his voice husky as he picked up a loose curl. Tiny particles of white fell to the ground as he rubbed the auburn lock between his thumb and forefinger, then tucked it behind her ear, the edge of his finger trailing along the sensitive shell. Eleanor's breath caught.

"So – so do you." Suddenly overwhelmed by an inexplicable shyness, she lowered her gaze to a silver button on his waistcoat. When Derek was rude and arrogant she knew what to say. How to act. What biting retort to give. But when he was like this…when his guard dropped away and she was given a rare glimpse at the man behind the hard wall of cynicism…she didn't have the faintest idea *what* she should do.

"I suppose we could take a bath," he drawled, and her startled gaze flew up to his countenance.

"T-together?" she stuttered even as heat pooled between her thighs like warm honey that had been left out in the sun. What would he look like naked, she wondered? All those hard lines and lean muscles, slick with water and covered in bubbles… She nibbled her lip and his eyes darkened.

"It might be a tight fit, but you could always sit on my lap. No?" he said when her cheeks pinkened and she gave a short, nervous giggle that sounded nothing at all like herself. "Then I suppose I can settle for a kiss..."

Nothing about the kiss was rehearsed or planned, and it was all the better for it. Eleanor gasped, both in surprise and sheer pleasure as he cupped the back of her head, the palms of his hands molding perfectly to the delicate curve of her skull, and took her mouth with his.

This time he was demanding instead of patient. Hard instead of soft. Fast instead of slow. He plundered her mouth without apology and she clung to him with all of the desperation of a sailor in the midst of a storm, her nails biting into his chest as he bit her lip.

His hands streaked down her back to cup her bottom through the thin fabric of her dress, squeezing the plump flesh until she moaned. The tiny, helpless little sound only seemed to fan the flames of his arousal, and with a feral growl he deepened the kiss, tongue plunging into her mouth as he yanked her against him.

Her entire body pulsed with heat. His radiated it. They were two suns colliding until suddenly, much like a storm that was there and then gone, leaving nothing but wrecked devastation in its wake, the kiss was over.

"Your pocket is growling at me," he said darkly.

"I...what?" Dazed and disoriented, it took Eleanor a moment to register what Derek was talking about. "Oh!" she said, her eyes widening when she belatedly remembered that Henny was still in her pocket. "Oh dear, I hope we haven't squished her!"

She scooped up the grumbling hedgehog, who appeared a tad disgruntled but otherwise unharmed. Sighing with relief, she nestled Henny against her chest and offered her husband an abashed smile. "Sorry about that. I forgot she was in there."

"Clearly." On a slow, measured breath he raked a hand through his hair, fingers drawing the ebony locks taut before letting them fall in a disheveled rumple. "Do you always keep an animal on your person?"

"Not *always*," she concluded after a pause, her head tilting to the side as she thought it over.

"That's a relief. I should hate to be poked or bitten in a sensitive area while attempting a passionate overture."

Eleanor blinked. Had he just…told a joke? To be honest, she didn't think him capable of humor. At least not the kind that was self-deprecating.

Her gaze softened as she studied him beneath her lashes. She liked him like this. Calm. Relaxed. Warm. After eleven months and ten days of marriage, she felt as if she was finally meeting her husband for the very first time. And he wasn't at all who she thought he was.

"What did you say to Mrs. Gibbons to make her leave in such a rush?" she asked curiously.

"I told her she was to be immediately relieved of all her duties," Derek said, speaking with the same air of nonchalance one used to discuss the weather instead of the dismissal of a loyal employee who had served his family for nearly three generations.

"You didn't," Eleanor gasped, her mouth dropping open.

"I certainly did." There wasn't a single flicker of

remorse in the deep, dark depths of his eyes. "She was disrespectful to my wife. I don't care what that damned goose of yours did. That sort of insolence will not be tolerated."

My wife.

She'd never heard him call her that before. It filled her with a secret thrill of delight even as guilt had her chewing on the inside of her cheek. "Mrs. Gibbons and I have had our differences, but I never wanted her to lose her position."

Derek snorted. "Mrs. Gibbons is an old dragon that has been terrorizing the staff for longer than I've been alive. She should have been retired a decade ago. Trust me. This is long overdue. She'll be more than fairly compensated for her service."

When he put it that way…

"Donald will certainly be relieved to know she is no longer at Hawkridge." She tucked a loose strand of hair behind her ear. It was the same curl Derek had rubbed between his fingers before he'd kissed her senseless.

Again.

She finally had an inkling for why a woman would act so silly over a man. Kissing was very nice. She dared say it was even better than crumpets. And she *really* loved crumpets.

Up until this moment, she'd always thought of their hasty wedding and the resulting marriage as a burden.

After all, she hadn't become a duchess because she *wanted* to. The title had been thrust upon her against her wishes, rather like the hideous purple turban her mother had made her wear to a ball once. Yes, Derek had left her alone and yes, she'd gotten everything she had ever wanted: a beautiful home in the country, abundant space for her animals, the freedom to do what she wanted when she wanted to do it. But lately she had begun to feel as if something was…lacking. She didn't know what it was, only that when Derek kissed her she felt fulfilled, like the something that was missing suddenly wasn't missing anymore.

"Would you like to meet the rest of them?" she asked.

"The rest of whom?" Using his sleeve, he wiped the remaining layer of flour off his face.

"My animals. They're all in the old carriage barn. Well, most of them," she amended with a glance down at Henny who had fallen asleep nestled against her chest. Derek lifted a brow.

"How many animals do you *have*?"

"You'll see," she said cheerfully. Tucking Henny back into her pocket, she hesitated for only a second before lightly wrapping her fingers around her husband's forearm when he offered it to her. Side by side, the Duke and Duchess of Hawkridge set off across the lawn towards the carriage barn.

CHAPTER ELEVEN

WHEN ELEANOR SAID 'ANIMALS', Derek had been expecting one or two geese and a cat. Not the entire menagerie of furred and feathered beasts that awaited him when his little wife slid open the door and gestured for him to quickly step in.

"The pygmy shrews have been trying to escape," she explained as she slid the door shut.

"Shrews?" Instantly wary, he stopped short and looked down at his feet. The floor of the barn was covered in a thick, sweet smelling layer of straw. Three wooden pens at the far end of the barn contained a trio of piglets, two geese – the infamous Ronald and his brother, he presumed – and twin lambs that were no bigger than a dinner plate. "You didn't say anything about shrews."

Her lips curved. "They're harmless. Although I would check your pockets before you go. They're always looking for a cozy place to nest."

Bloody hell.

"Perhaps this was a bad idea." He started edging towards the door. "I'll come back when the rats, er, shrews are all properly contained. I wouldn't want to step on one."

"Then I would suggest you stop moving." One glance at his face and her smile widened. "Your Grace?" she said sweetly.

"Yes?" Derek muttered as he continued to search the straw.

"Are you afraid of pygmy shrews?"

"Afraid of – no," he said, looking up at her with a scowl. "What an absurd thing to suggest."

"You certainly *look* rather afraid," she pointed out. "If you'd like, you can go stand on that chair. They shouldn't be able to reach you there."

The chair was tempting, but he wasn't about to go leaping up on furniture like a frightened school girl. "I don't need a chair," he said, folding his arms across his chest. "And I am not afraid of pygmy shrews." His voice lowered. "I'm afraid of rats."

It was a silly weakness he'd never admitted to anyone before. Mostly because he knew that if his grandfather found out, he would have teased him mercilessly. Or – even worse – put rats in his shoes. Which was precisely where he'd discovered one when he was eight years old, and why he still loathed the beady-eyed creatures to this day.

"Well I can assure you there are no rats in here. They chew," she explained when he looked at her suspiciously. "And they're constantly getting into the grain in the horse stables. Whereas pygmy shrews only eat insects and insect larvae. Oh look! There's one now."

With all the speed and precision of a cat pouncing on a mouse, she dropped to her knees in the straw and cupped her hands together. She rose slowly to her feet; a duchess with straw in her hair and a pygmy shrew trapped between her palms. A beam of morning light swept in through a window, illuminating the dusty gold smattering of freckles across her nose and turning her tousled mane from deep red to burnished copper. It spilled over her shoulders in a wave of curls that glowed like fire against her porcelain skin.

"You're beautiful," he said, staring at her in astonishment. How had he not seen it before? Perhaps because her beauty was nothing like Vanessa's cool, reserved prettiness. Eleanor wasn't a finely tended rose kept under glass. She was a wildflower growing in an untended field. Her petals weren't perfect. Her leaves were a bit frayed. But all of her imperfections only made her that much more stunning.

Straw rustled under his boots as he started to step closer to her, possessed by the sudden urge to gather her in his arms and twist his fingers through those glorious curls and kiss every imperfect freckle scattered across her cheeks.

Then he remembered the rat.

"Don't worry." Mistaking his approach for interest in the pygmy shrew that was poking its twitching nose out between her fingers, Eleanor smiled and held up her hands. "Bianca doesn't bite."

"Bianca?" he questioned, one brow lifting.

"Yes. I named all of them after characters from Shakespeare's *Taming of the Shrew*."

Every muscle in his body stilled. "*All* of them? How many are there?"

"Only four."

Only four. He barely managed to restrain a snort. She might as well have said there were only four horsemen of the apocalypse.

"Hold out your hands," Eleanor instructed.

Derek blinked. "I'll do no such thing."

"I promise she won't bite. Bianca is a lady. Aren't you?" she cooed, nuzzling the shrew's tiny nose. Her laughing gaze flicked to her husband. "Come now. There's nothing to be afraid of."

His shoulders stiffened. "I'm not afraid."

"Then prove it."

Of course she would call him out. Any other woman – or man, for that matter – would have known enough to respect his wishes when he made them clear the first time. Then again, Eleanor wasn't like any other woman he'd ever met before. Before he had returned to Hawkridge he'd always seen her peculiarities as flaws. Things to be ignored instead of encouraged. But now he wasn't beginning to wonder if her uniqueness wasn't the most special thing about her.

"Fine," he said grudgingly as he held out his hands.

"Closer together and cup your fingers. Yes, like that. Are you ready?"

No.

"Just do it," he said, gritting his teeth and looking past her to the far wall. He held his breath when he felt a slight weight drop into his palms. Let it out in a slow, controlled hiss of air when whiskers brushed against his skin. Gazing down, he found himself staring at one of the smallest creatures he'd ever seen. Covered in sleek brown fur with a hairless tail and a pointed nose, Bianca the pygmy shrew was smaller than the length of his thumb. She wandered to the edge of his hand, peered down at the long drop below, and promptly turned back around.

"Isn't she adorable?" Eleanor beamed, their shoulders brushing as she positioned herself beside him so they could look down at Bianca together.

Yes, he thought silently, although he wasn't looking at the shrew. *She certainly is.*

"I found the entire litter washed up in the field. That happens sometimes after a hard rain. Their mother was nowhere to be found, so I brought them back here. They're almost ready to be released."

Eleanor's enthusiasm was contagious, and despite his earlier reservations he found himself warming to the miniature rodent with the long whiskers and pointy snout. "And your other animals?" he asked, nodding towards the pigs and the lambs and the geese, all of which had settled down for a mid-morning nap. "How did you manage to find those?"

"Well I..." she hesitated. "Do you *really* want to know?"

"Yes," he said, surprising himself. "I really do."

"All right. Then let's start with Sir Galahad and Lancelot..."

One by one she introduced him to her pets. Most of them would be released into the wild or given back to their owners, she explained, but some – like the pigs, who had been turned away from their mother at birth – she was afraid to return to the farmer for fear of finding them on the dinner menu.

"You're going to need a bigger barn soon." Carefully transferring Bianca back to her adopted mother, Derek rested his hands on his hips and turned in a slow circle. "Not to mention the fact that this building should have been demolished last year. Do you see the beams there, how they're leaning to the side? That's only going to get worse. It's not safe."

"But there's nowhere else for the animals to go," Eleanor protested. Returning the pygmy shrew to a square wooden box, she joined her husband in studying the interior of the dilapidated barn. "I know it's a little worn, but all of the other outbuildings are being utilized. This was the only one that was free."

"Then we'll build another," he said matter-of-factly.

Derek considered himself to be a generous man – when the occasion suited. Over the years he'd spent a significant fortune on presents for his various mistresses. Diamond necklaces. Ruby bracelets. Emerald earrings. He gave them priceless pieces of jewelry not because he necessarily wanted to, but because it was expected of him. When one kept a mistress it was what one did. And they'd all shown their appreciation in a myriad of creative (and pleasurable) ways. But not a single mistress had ever looked at him like Eleanor was looking at him now.

"Really?" she whispered, her eyes as bright and wide as he'd ever seen them and filled with gratitude. One glance into those green shimmering pools and a man would be lucky if he didn't lose himself forever. "You would do that for me?"

I would hang the stars for you.

The foolishly romantic thought, far better suited to a

dreamy eyed poet than a cynical duke, made him scowl. Where the devil had *that* come from? Furthermore, why was he standing ankle-deep in straw learning all about pygmy shrews when he should have been in his study catching up on a year's worth of correspondences?

The country air was clearly getting to his head. It was the only damn thing that made any sense. The sooner he returned to London the better. Then he could focus on finding a new mistress. One who didn't defy him or run around the lawn chasing after geese or forget to wear bonnets.

"It wouldn't be for you, it would be for the estate," he said brusquely. "

The light in Eleanor's eyes dimmed. "I see," she said, trying – and failing – to mimic his cold, businesslike tone. There was nothing cold or businesslike about her. From her Titian curls to her red hot temper, she was all heat. "Well either way, my animals will be appreciative. I'd like to speak to the foreman before he begins construction. I have several ideas that I think–"

"No," he said abruptly.

"No?" Her eyebrows drew together. "No to what?"

"All of it. All of this." He gestured to the wooden pens with a short, agitated sweep of his arm. "You are not an architect or an animal doctor. You're a duchess. And it's time you began acting like one." In the back of his mind Derek knew he was being a right bastard, but he didn't care. It was better to be angry than weak. Better to think of his wife as a means to an end rather than the means to a beginning. He'd come here to consummate his marriage and save Hawkridge from his cousin. Not fall head over heels for a wild hellion with straw in her hair and a hedgehog in her pocket

I would hang the stars for you.

Bloody hell. If his grandfather ever heard him spouting off such utter twaddle the old man would laugh himself right out of his grave.

"What is *that* supposed to mean?" Eleanor demanded.

"It means your days of tromping around the estate like an uncivilized savage are at an end. You belong in the ballroom, not the barn. I'll hire a tenant farmer to care for the animals and you will start attending to your duties as the Duchess of Hawkridge."

Heat flashed in her eyes as her tiny hands curled into fists. Sensing her growing ire, one of the geese – Donald? – let out a startled honk. "These are *my* animals and *I* will care for them. You have no right to tell me what to do!"

"That's where you're wrong, Red," he said silkily. "As your husband, I have *every* right. You belong to me as much as this barn and the land it sits upon does."

If her gaze was any hotter he would have been

incinerated where he stood. "I don't belong to anyone, least of all a pompous, egotistical husband who should have remained in London!" Her skirts swished furiously as she advanced on him and jabbed a finger at the middle of his chest. "Why couldn't you have stayed away? No one wants you here!"

The barb was a cruel one made all the sharper by the ghosts of his past.

No one wants you here.

You're worthless.

You'll never amount to anything.

His teeth clenched, sending a fissure of tension radiating through his jaw and into his skull. He captured her wrist before she could drill her finger into his chest again, fingers closing around bones that were as slender and slight as the wing of a bird. How could something so delicate contain so much fire? Staring down into her flashing gaze he was tempted to kiss her, just to see what all that fire and fury would taste like.

"Be that as it may," he ground out, "I am the duke, and as such my word is law. You *will* obey me. Is that understood?"

"The only thing I understand," Eleanor sneered, "is that I *never* should have married you. Go to hell, Derek! Maybe you'll find an obedient wife there." Snatching her wrist free she turned on her heel and stormed out, slamming the door behind her with so much force the entire barn trembled.

Chapter Twelve

If anything good came of Eleanor and Derek's spat in the barn, it was that Derek stopped his campaign of flowery compliments and meaningless gifts.

When they passed one another in the hallway they each looked straight ahead, refusing to acknowledge the other's existence. Choosing which room to occupy became a battle strategy, with Eleanor laying claim to the front drawing room and the library while Derek stayed mostly in his study and the gaming room. Dinner was a frigid affair, with neither one speaking a word. If not for Georgiana's careless prattle they would have eaten in complete silence.

So it went for the better part of a week…until the night everything changed.

Awakening with a start, Eleanor sat bolt upright in bed and clutched the sheets to her chest as she looked wildly around the room, wondering what had woken her. She had her answer a few seconds later when a thunderous booming *crash* shook the windows.

Rain lashed against the glass in pounding sheets and when a jagged streak of white lightning raced across the sky it illuminated the entire room. Throwing her blankets aside, Eleanor slid out of bed and dashed to the nearest window. She'd always been drawn to the magnetic power of storms. There was something almost otherworldly about them, and when she was a child learning about Greek mythology she'd believed – at least for a time – they were the result of Zeus' wrathful temper.

Pressing her nose against the cool glass, she eagerly awaited the next boom of thunder. When it struck it seemed to shake the entire house, from the rafters to the floor boards. Grinning ear to ear, she jumped back and glanced at the foot of the bed where Henny liked to burrow.

"Henny, did you hear that? It sounded like – Henny?" Concern tempered her excitement when she realized the little hedgehog wasn't in her usual spot. Another flash of lightning lit up the room as she returned to the bed and looked under the blankets and pillows, but her pet was nowhere to be found. Frightened by the noise, she must have scurried off while Eleanor still slept.

"Henny!" Dropping to her hands and knees, Eleanor began a frantic search of the room. She was wedged halfway under the bed, rump in the air and nose burrowed in a ball of cat hair, when she heard the door creak open.

"This looks alarmingly familiar," Derek drawled as he walked into her bedchamber. "Please tell me you're not stuck again."

"I'm not stuck. I'm – *ow!*" she hissed when she hit her head on one of the wooden slats. Rubbing the injured area, she managed to scuttle sideways out from under the bed and clambered to her feet to glare at the duke. "I'm looking for Henny. The storm scared her and she's run away."

"Henny…Henny…" he said thoughtfully, rubbing his chin. He hadn't shaved in the past two days, allowing a scruff of dark shadow to grow along the lower half of his face. It made him look less like a duke and more like a pirate, one whom Eleanor hoped was going to return to the sea very, very soon. "Short, round woman? Prickly demeanor? Enjoys grubs and crumpets? You know, I never thought of it before, but aside from your physical attributes and the grubs – which are utterly disgusting, by the way – you and that hedgehog of yours have quite a bit in common."

"Ha ha," Eleanor bit out sarcastically. "If you've come in here just to insult me–"

"I came in here," he interrupted, "to deliver a special gift."

She'd been wondering if he would try to bribe his

way back into her good graces with a pretty – and completely useless – piece of jewelry. She might have even been swayed to forgive him…*if* the gesture was genuine. But since she knew it wasn't, she had no interest in accepting a fancy bauble just so he could appease his conscience. If he even had a conscience. After their argument in the carriage barn she was beginning to have her doubts.

"I don't want an apology necklace or bracelet," she said, squaring her shoulders.

"Would you settle for an apology hedgehog?" And with a showy flourish he dipped his hand into the pocket of his waistcoat and pulled out a very sleepy looking Henny. With a big yawn the little hedgehog turned around once, twice, and then curled up in a ball in the middle of Derek's palm. Eleanor's mouth dropped open.

"Where did you find her?" she gasped.

"Tickling my ear, if you must know. I thought for a moment my wife had come to make midnight amends." His teeth flashed wolfishly in the darkness. "Imagine my disappointment when I rolled over and found my bedmate had quills."

"Thank you for bringing her to me." Ignoring the tiny quiver in her belly as she wondered just what sort of 'midnight amends' her husband had in mind, she walked purposefully across the room and gently lifted Henny out of his hand.

Pressing a kiss upon the top of her pet's head – while most hedgehogs were nocturnal, Henny had long ago adapted to Eleanor's schedule – she deposited her in a wicker basket with a lid that hooked closed so Henny couldn't go on anymore nighttime excursions. Tucking the basket into a closet where the sounds of thunder would be muffled, she turned back towards Derek just as another brilliant streak of lightning lit up the room.

The blinding flash of white illuminated the duke's countenance, and even though it only lasted for a split second it was long enough for Eleanor to see the dark desire in her husband's gaze. Her breath caught in her throat as he prowled towards her, his steps as long and fluid as a panther, his ebony hair just as sleek and his eyes…his eyes glowing with a feral intensity she'd never seen before.

"What – what are you doing?" she asked, swallowing nervously. A quick glance over her shoulder revealed there was nowhere for her to go as he advanced with a single-minded purpose. In four strides she was pinned against the chaise longue, the back of her knees pushing against the sumptuous velvet as she leaned away from him.

"Something I should have done a long time ago."

"K-kiss me?" she ventured.

"That's a good place to start." As thunder boomed and lightning flashed, Derek buried his hands in her unruly waterfall of auburn curls, tilted her head back, and plundered her mouth with his. After a moment of token hesitation – she may have been angry with him, but she so *did* enjoy kissing him – Eleanor parted her lips and welcomed the slide of his tongue into the dark recesses of her mouth.

This kiss wasn't like the others. She sensed that at once. There was intention behind it. A thrilling sense of something more to come. It was the beginning, not the middle. And not nearly close to the end.

Her small hands splayed across his granite chest, fingers slipping beneath his open waistcoat to brush against the soft fabric of his shirt. Beneath the ivory linen she felt his muscles coil and clench, and her belly did the same when he cupped her breasts through the lace-trimmed bodice of her pale blue nightdress. His thumbs flicked across her dusky nipples and her head fell back, green eyes bright and glassy as she stared blindly up at the ceiling.

"Do you like it when I touch you like this?" he murmured, his voice a velvet rasp of sinful decadence against her flesh before he took her earlobe between his teeth and suckled. Incapable of speech she managed a jerky nod, and felt the rumble of husky laughter against her neck.

"I'm going to touch you everywhere before we're done. Here." He squeezed her breast. "And here." His hand trailed with tantalizing slowness down to her navel. "And especially here." He cupped her womanhood and she gasped, her startled gaze flying to his face.

Biologically she knew how intercourse worked. She'd read enough books on the subject to glean the basic mechanics of it all. Granted, they'd mostly been about animals, but procreation was procreation. The man's genitalia went into the female's genitalia and semen was released. On paper, it was all very matter-of-fact and to the point. But this wasn't paper. Which was a very good thing, she thought dazedly, for if it were they'd surely burn the entire house down.

He gave a light flick of his finger and heat bloomed between her thighs. Another flick and her knees wobbled. Shamelessly she spread her legs apart, her body instinctively yearning for more pleasure. She may have been a virgin inexperienced in the art of lovemaking, but she knew what she liked. And she was bold enough to ask for it.

"What a greedy little temptress you are." Derek captured her mouth again, taking long, slow pulls that mimicked the stroking of his finger as it burrowed deeper and deeper between her nest of curls, seeking – and finding – the most intimate part of her through the thin layer of her nightdress.

She groaned when he abruptly withdrew his hand.

Trembled when he began to kiss his way down her neck. Shivered when his clever fingers caught on the shoulders of her nightdress and slowly pulled it down until her breasts, pale as freshly fallen snow in the intermittent darkness, spilled free.

Once the nightdress slithered past her hips it fell in a pool of white cotton at her feet. Embarrassment at being naked brought a dull flush of red to her chest and cheeks, but any discomfort was immediately forgotten when he picked her up and then gently lowered her onto the bed.

Reclining back on a small mountain of pillows she watched through heavily lidded eyes as he undressed, starting with his waistcoat and ending with his trousers. Her eyes widened when she saw *that* part of him, smooth and pulsing and so large that if it weren't for all of the books she'd read she never would have believed it was going to fit inside of her. As it stood she had her doubts, but they drifted away in a cloud of sensual pleasure when he lowered his body onto hers and began to kiss every inch of her until she was half mad with need and writhing with desire.

Outside the windows the storm raged on, a wild tempest that paled in comparison to the raw strength of their passion. Reaching down to the floor, Derek yanked up his trousers and pulled a small glass vial no larger than a pill box out of one pocket.

"What's that?" Eleanor asked, sitting up on her elbows to watch in fascination as he unscrewed the top of the vial and poured its contents into his palm.

"Olive oil. It will help ease the pain of your first time." He kept his gaze steady on hers as he slathered his cock with the oil, then positioned himself on top of her. "Look at me," he whispered when his hand, still slick with oil, dipped between her legs. He used two fingers to slowly and carefully ready her entrance, circling, stroking, stretching as she bit down hard on her bottom lip and wondered if it was possible for a person to spontaneously combust into flame. "Keep your eyes only on me."

Then he was sinking into her and at first she felt only pressure and the tiniest twinge of pain, but soon there was only wave after wave of undulating pleasure as he began to plunge deeper and deeper with every roll of his hips.

Thunder crashed. Lightning erupted. And they both tumbled off the edge into oblivion.

Chapter Thirteen

"Why are you looking at me like that?" Eleanor asked, one auburn brow arching.

"Like what?" Derek replied, absently twirling a sprig of clover between his fingers. The clover was the same color as her eyes, a deep emerald that reminded him of the rolling hills of Scotland right before the heather took bloom and everything was dark and rich and green.

It had been precisely thirteen days since their marriage had finally been consummated, but it already felt like a lifetime…in the best possible way. They spent every night wrapped in each other's arms and every afternoon, after Eleanor had tended to her animals and he'd seen to his work, they explored the estate like children, each day seeking a new and exciting adventure.

Thus far they had gone galloping through the fields on horseback, climbed to the top of the highest turret, played a rousing game of chess in the library, and taken a (very cold) midnight dip in the pond sans clothing. Today they'd packed a picnic basket and taken an early dinner on one of the side lawns overlooking the horse pastures where a herd of mares and their foals frolicked and played.

Through Eleanor's eyes he had begun to see Hawkridge in a new light. When he was with her the ghosts of his past faded away and he was able to appreciate the castle for what it was now instead of loathing what it had been.

Instead of a prison, he saw promise. Instead of inconvenience, he saw opportunity. And instead of a wife he wanted to forget, he saw a woman he always wanted to remember.

"Like you don't hate me," she said, leaning forward to pluck another piece of roasted chicken out of the basket. Ignoring the utensils a maid had thoughtfully packed, she ate with her bare hands, nibbling the chicken down to the bone before tossing the scraps to the two pigs that had followed them on their little excursion and were now sitting side by side like expertly trained dogs.

"I don't hate you." Derek's stomach clenched unpleasantly. Is that what she still thought? That he hated her? He supposed he couldn't blame her, given the monstrous way he'd behaved. He'd called Eleanor a savage, but in truth *he* was the barbaric one. By forcing himself to see her as nothing more than a means to an end, he had treated her with unnecessary cruelty. Cruelty that he now regretted down to the depths of his soul.

He'd tried to make up for his behavior the same way he always had: with expensive gifts. His mistresses had always forgiven him any transgression – real or imaginary – for a pretty piece of glitter. But his wife had gently declined each and every present he tried to give her.

'I don't need jewelry or furs or fancy dresses,' she told him one morning when they'd lain sprawled on their backs on top of the coverlet, their bodies covered with a thin sheen of perspiration after making love as the sun rose in the east. *'I would much rather have time.'*

'Time?' he'd asked, his brow furrowing.

'Time with you. Time with my animals. Time with myself. Time is more special than all the jewels in the world because it can never be bought, only given. Give me time, and I shall be the happiest woman in the world'.

So that's what he'd done. He had given her time. It was the least expensive – albeit the most important – gift he had ever bestowed.

Their marriage was still far from perfect. They'd had

an argument just that morning about where the new carriage barn was going to be built. And even though he had walked away in a fit of anger – Eleanor knew *exactly* what strings to pull to get under his skin – he had quickly returned. He would *always* return. Because for the first time in his life, he'd allowed a relationship to become personal. And it may not have been perfect or easy, but that was what made it so right.

"I've never hated you," he continued, his gaze seeking and finding hers. "It's just that…I was never expecting you. I wasn't adequately prepared."

A smile hovered in the corners of her mouth. "You make me sound like a storm."

"Yes," he said without hesitation. "That's precisely what you are."

Her smile was replaced with a perplexed frown. "Well that doesn't sound very good. No one likes storms. They're disruptive and damaging."

"Yes," he repeated. "They are. But sometimes they're exactly what's needed to wash away the old and make way for the new. Without storms we wouldn't have lightning or thunder or the wild rush of cool rain on a hot summer's night. Without storms nature would be dull and meaningless. One day running into the next with nothing to break up the monotony of it all." Leaning over the basket he gently cupped her cheek and lowered his mouth to hers. "You're my storm Eleanor," he murmured against her lips. "And I wouldn't have you any other way."

On a soft, dreamy sigh Eleanor leaned into the kiss.

A storm, she thought with no small amount of delight as Derek nibbled lazily at her bottom lip. It was the least complimentary compliment he'd ever given her. And all the more perfect because of it.

If someone told her she and the duke would be kissing over a picnic supper less than one month after his return to Hawkridge, she would have laughed herself into a fit. Yet here they were, sitting in the middle of the lawn with a basket between them and Sir Galahad and Lancelot chaperoning from a distance.

The last two weeks had been the most magical of her life. Not because she had discovered lovemaking – well, not *only* because she'd discovered lovemaking – but because she had finally discovered her husband. It may have taken eleven months and twenty-nine days, but at long last she'd found the man behind the mask. And he was everything she ever could have hoped for.

Gone was the cad who had mocked her and demanded she give up her animals. In his place was the man who had given her her very first kiss. The valiant knight who had saved Donald from the housekeeper and rescued Henny from the thunderstorm. The charming rogue who had, against all odds, managed to steal her heart.

All that being said, he was still a scoundrel and they still fought like cats and dogs. But that was part of their appeal. Despite what he'd said in the carriage barn out of anger, Derek did not want her to be anyone other than who she was. He told her as much the morning after they'd made love when the first light of dawn had yet to steal across the sky and she'd been tucked into the hard concave of his body.

'You're not like anyone I've ever met before,' he'd told her, one hand absently combing through her tangled curls. *'I used to think that was a bad thing. But now I know it's your greatest asset. Never change, Eleanor. Even if someone is stupid enough to ask you to.'*

To date, it was the second best compliment he'd ever given her.

"We need to stop," she murmured, pushing lightly against his chest when she felt his fingers unbuttoning the back of her dress.

"Why?" he asked as his lips worked their way down her throat.

"Because…because I think I hear someone coming up the drive."

"Let them come. I certainly intend to," he said, mouth curving in a wicked grin against her bare shoulder as he pulled her sleeve down. She batted his hand away.

"Derek, I'm serious."

"So am I. Fine," he sighed. Giving her one last kiss, he stood up and shrugged on his waistcoat. "But if this is anyone less than the king himself, I'm coming back here and – *bloody hell*."

"What?" Alarmed by the dark shadow that stole across his countenance as he turned to look at the drive and the shiny black coach rolling up it, Eleanor scrambled to her feet and hastily straightened her bodice. "Do you know who that is?" she asked, watching as a tall, thin man alighted from the carriage and, after a surreptitious glance at the manor, proceeded directly inside.

"Yes," Derek said grimly.

"And?"

"You're better off not knowing. This will only take a few minutes."

"I'll go with you." She started to follow him, but he stopped so abruptly she nearly ran into him.

"It's better if you remain here."

"But I–"

"Eleanor." His jaw tensed. "Please."

"Very well," she said, even though she had absolutely no intention of staying put. "But only if you promise to tell me who that man is when you return."

He pressed a distracted kiss to her brow. "I promise."

She waited until he'd gone around the front of the

house before she picked up her skirts and dashed around the back. Using the servant's entrance, she slipped through the kitchens and down the hall.

It was easy to find where her husband had gone. All she had to do was follow the sound of raised voices to the front drawing room. The door had been left slightly ajar and she felt only the slightest twinge of guilt as she peeked inside. If Derek hadn't wanted her to eavesdrop then he should have at least told her who the man was that had instantly put him in such a bad mood. It wasn't *her* fault she had a healthy dose of curiosity.

Her husband stood with his back to her, his rugged frame partially obscuring the thin stranger so all she saw was one sharp blue eye and a flattened lick of black hair. Georgiana, dressed in black and looking supremely bored, sat on the sofa with Mr. Pumpernickel perched on her lap. Over the past few weeks the two had taken a liking to one another and it was rare to see them apart.

"...know you're not welcome here, Norton," said Derek tersely. She couldn't see his face, but his tension was obvious in the rigid line of his shoulders.

"I'm family, aren't I?" The stranger – Norton – replied with an insolent sneer that immediately put a bad taste in Eleanor's mouth. If he really was family it must have been a distant relation, for with the exception of their hair color he and Derek looked *nothing* alike.

"You should have sent a calling card, dear cousin."

This from Georgiana who was looking at Norton as if he were something she'd just had scraped off the bottom of her shoe. "At least then we would have known to hide the silver."

"Georgie. Pleasant as ever, I see." Norton's attention flicked back to Derek. He smiled thinly. "You know very well why I'm here. The timing of the will was quite specific."

The will? Eleanor's brow knitted with confusion. What will?

"With one day to go, I decided to see for myself if you've met the terms our dearly departed grandfather set forth. I wish it didn't have to come to this, Derek. Truly I don't." Norton's sigh was annoyingly long. "But the will was quite clear, I'm afraid."

"I know the bloody terms of the will," Derek snapped. "Say what you've come to say and then get the hell out. My patience is wearing thin."

"Very well. I hesitate to speak so bluntly in front of a lady." His gaze swerved back to Georgiana as an insolent smirk twisted his narrow lips. "Which is why I'm glad there isn't one here."

A growl that was more beast than man tore bubbled up from Derek's throat. "Insult my sister again," he said in a deceptively soft voice, "and it will be the last thing you do."

"What's a little teasing between family? Fine, fine,"

he said when Derek took a menacing step in his direction. "No need to get violent. No need at all. *This* is why Grandfather put that last little caveat in the will, you know. Because he knew you weren't suited to be a duke. You haven't the temperament for it."

"You'd have Hawkridge run into the ground before the year was out," Georgiana said disdainfully. "Everyone knows you're out of money, Norton. And desperate enough to do anything to get your hands on my brother's inheritance. I almost feel sorry for you."

"Save your pity for yourself when I toss you out on your ear," Norton spat as his face blanched and then turned a deep, dull red. "Enough of these games. The will was clear, and it will hold up in any court. So has the marriage been consummated or not? You've only two days left."

Eleanor concealed her gasp just in time. Clapping a hand over her mouth, she stared at her husband in shocked silence as she began to understand just what Norton was talking about. There was a will, created by the late Duke of Hawkridge, Derek's grandfather. And within in it he must have made some sort of stipulation that Derek had to marry before his twenty-ninth birthday. She didn't know exactly what would happen if he didn't meet the terms of the will…but it wasn't hard to guess. The title would pass to the next male heir, in this case Norton.

Was *that* why Derek had returned to Hawkridge? To consummate their marriage and make it legally binding? Had he been plotting to get her into his bed this entire time? Had the last two weeks meant nothing to him?

As she thought of every loving word and every gentle touch they'd exchanged, she felt a hard knot form in the middle of her chest. *Lies*, she thought as she reeled away from the door. It had all been nothing but one lie after another. Derek didn't care for her. He never had. He simply hadn't wanted to lose the dukedom. And as soon as he told his cousin the terms of the will had been met in full, he was going to return to London and she would never see him again.

With a muffled sob she turned on her heel and fled down the hall.

AT THE SOUND of a soft cry, Derek whirled around. Biting back a savage curse when he saw a flash of Eleanor's blue dress as she bolted away from the door, he immediately went after her. He could hear Norton shouting something at him, but his cousin's whiny voice paled in comparison the dull roaring in his ears.

"See that my cousin is immediately escorted off the property," he told the first footman he came across. "And if he tries to return, shoot him."

With that matter finished, he set off to find Eleanor. Knowing a search of the house would prove futile, he went immediately to the old carriage barn. She'd barred the door against him, but with one kick of his boot he sent it crashing open.

"Get out!" Eleanor she cried when he stepped inside, dashing at her cheeks as she rose from the pile of straw she'd been crouched in. Donald and Ronald stood on either side of her, their necks arched and their feathers raised. "I have nothing to say to you."

"I know what you think you heard," he began in a low, soothing tone. "But you have to let me explain–"

"Did you or did you not come here with the sole purpose of consummating our marriage so you wouldn't lose your title to your cousin?" she demanded hotly.

"Yes, that's why I came here," he admitted, and pain sliced through him like a dagger to the heart when her bottom lip wobbled. He took a step towards her. Would have taken another if not for Donald and Ronald's low warning hiss. Damned geese. The things were more dangerous than a pair of wolfhounds. "That's why I came here," he repeated, lifting his arms beseechingly. "But it's not why I stayed."

With an incredulous snort she turned her head to the side, refusing to meet his gaze.

"Eleanor, look at me," he said softly. "Please. It's not what you think."

Tears shimmered in her eyes as she glared fiercely at him. It was the first time he had ever seen her cry, and his heart ached anew to know that he was the cause of all her pain. If only he'd explained the bloody will before now…but things had been going so well he'd been reluctant to bring it up for fear of this exact reaction.

"I thought – I thought you were falling in love with me," she whispered.

"I *am* falling in love with you." His hands curled into fists. "I *have* fallen in love with you."

"No you haven't," she said, shaking her head from side to side. "It was all a ruse. An act. You played me like a fool, and the worst thing is that I let you do it."

"If you would just – dammit!" he exclaimed when he tried to get closer to her and one of the geese lashed out. "Call off your guard dogs, Red. Let me explain."

Reaching into a metal bin, she picked up a handful of corn and tossed it behind her into the straw. "There," she said as Ronald and Donald waddled away. "Now you can explain."

"You're right about the will. I discovered the terms shortly after my grandfather died and I inherited everything. My relationship with him was…let's just say it was tumultuous. He knew the last thing I wanted to do was marry, at least before I turned thirty, and so that was the one thing he forced me to do." Derek's mouth twisted in a bitter smile. "He also knew I would never allow Hawkridge to go to Norton. As you saw for yourself, the conniving little bastard is even worse than I am."

"I wouldn't go that far," Eleanor muttered under her breath. "Was it all planned then, from the very beginning?"

"No." In two strides he was standing directly in front of her. Reaching out, he brushed his thumb across her damp cheek, catching a tear before it could roll down her chin. "You were never planned, Eleanor. I know I haven't been a good husband to you. I know you have no reason to believe me, other than the fact that I have no reason to lie. So know that I speak the absolute truth when I tell you that you were never the wife I wanted. But you were always the wife I needed," he murmured into her hair as he wrapped his arms around her and pulled her gently against his chest. "I'm just so bloody sorry it took me a damned year to realize it."

"Eleven months and fifteen days," she said, her voice muffled against his chest.

"What?" he said with a frown.

"Eleven months and fifteen days. That's exactly how long it took you to realize that you're hopelessly, helplessly in love with me." When she tipped back her head all of her tears were gone and she was smiling the brightest, most beautiful smile he had ever seen. At the sight of it he exhaled the breath he hadn't even realized he'd been holding and tightened his grip.

"Do you forgive me then?" he asked, gazing down into her brilliant green eyes. Green eyes that were filled with more love and understanding than he had any right to deserve. "I know I should have told you about the will sooner. I was an idiot not to."

"Yes," she agreed. "You were. But I do forgive you. On *one* condition."

"Anything," he said instantly.

"Henny has been feeling rather lonely lately–"

"No," he said, already shaking his head. "That hedgehog has already caused enough damage. We're not getting another."

"*That* hedgehog is the only reason we're together," she countered.

When she put it that way…

"Very well. You can have as many hedgehogs as your heart desires." Lifting her chin, he grinned crookedly down into her beaming face. "But only if you kiss me first."

With a musical laugh, she threw her arms around his neck. "I thought you'd never ask…"

Epilogue

4 years, 9 months, and 11 days later...

"Mum! Mum! They're hatching! They're hatching! Come *quickly*." Grabbing onto her mother's wrist with surprising strength given her diminutive size, four-year-old Olivia dragged a laughing Eleanor out of the drawing room and into the foyer.

"You'll need a hat and cloak," Eleanor told her daughter sternly. "It's cold outside."

"But it's spring." Olivia's freckled nose scrunched up in defiance. "And *you* never wear a hat."

Stubborn little brat, Eleanor thought with great affection. Olivia may have inherited her father's dark hair, but her freckles and opinionated nature came straight from her mother.

"I will this time." Reaching into the closet, Eleanor pulled out the first hat she could find, a straw Capote trimmed with blue ribbon and white silk flowers. "There," she said, adjusting the wide brim so it was centered over her forehead. "What do you think?"

"I think you're the most beautiful woman I've ever

seen," Derek drawled as he entered the foyer and kissed his wife's cheek before looping his arm around her waist and tucking her snugly against his side. "Where are my two favorite ladies off to on this fine morning?"

"The eggs are hatching!" Olivia exclaimed, her ebony curls bouncing as she jumped up and down with excitement.

"Are they?" said Derek with wide-eyed surprise. "Well then, this is a very serious occasion indeed. Shall I call for the trumpets?"

The corners of her mouth twitching, Eleanor slanted her husband an amused glance. Nearly six years married and he never failed to make her smile each and every day. She'd thought she was in love with him before their children were born, but it was nothing compared to what she felt for him now.

When her belly was heavy with Olivia he'd confessed to her that he was afraid of what sort of father he would be. Having lost his own at such a young age, he had only his grandfather for comparison, a man whom Eleanor was very glad she never had the occasion to meet.

'I very nearly ruined our marriage,' he said, brandy eyes dark with worry. *'What if I ruin our child? What if he or she despises me?'*

'Just be yourself,' she told him before taking his hand and pressing it to her abdomen. *'There, do you feel*

that strong kick? Our baby loves you already. All you have to do is love him or her in return.'

And he had. First Olivia and then Byron, now eight months old and growing like a weed. Fatherhood had also had the added benefit of making him an even better husband. Gone was the arrogant cad she'd married. In his place was a man who valued family first and foremost. A man who understood what was important in life. A man who finally knew that love wasn't an inconvenience, but a gift. The most precious gift a person could give or receive.

They still argued, of course. They were both too stubborn not to. But they always made up in the most delicious of ways, and Eleanor was fairly certain one of their latest arguments was going to yield a wonderful surprise in the coming months. It was still too early to know with absolute certainty, but she had a feeling. The same wonderful, glowing feeling she'd had with Olivia and Byron. That, coupled with the fact that she'd tossed up a perfectly good blueberry scone this morning, made her almost positive she was carrying their third child.

"Oh, I don't think there's time for trumpets," she said, looking at Derek with mock seriousness. "Best we get down to the pond as quick as we can."

"Before all of the eggs hatch!" Olivia shouted, clapping her hands with glee.

"Precisely. Have you seen your brother and Mrs.

Faraday?" she asked, referring to the children's nanny, a sweet woman in her mid-forties who had the patience of a saint, a necessary requirement when dealing with a very stubborn four-year-old.

"She just took Byron to the nursery for *another* nap." Olivia's hands dropped to her waist as she rolled her eyes. "Babies sleep a lot."

"That they do, half pint." Derek ruffled his daughter's hair. "That they do. As soon as you put on a hat like your mother instructed, we can go see if the eggs have hatched."

Olivia, who wouldn't hesitate to stand and argue with her mother until her face turned blue, promptly dove into the closet and pulled out both a bonnet and a cloak. Shaking her head at the irony – how as it *she'd* been the one forced to endure eighteen hours of labor, but it was *Derek* the children obeyed without fail? – Eleanor helped her daughter dress before swatting her on the rump and sending her out the door. While she ran ahead the duke and duchess followed at a more leisurely pace.

"I'm glad you didn't go to London this week," she said, flicking Derek a warm glance from beneath her lashes. While she'd made Hawkridge Castle her permanent residence and only went into town once a year to celebrate Christmas with her parents, a tradition they'd started after Olivia was born, Derek made the short trip twice a month to meet with his solicitor and visit Georgiana, who had settled quite nicely into a townhouse on the edge of Grosvenor Square. Despite their initial misgivings towards one another, she and Eleanor now exchanged regular letters. As soon as the Season was complete she would be returning to Hawkridge for the summer.

"And miss all the excitement?" Derek grinned down at her and shook his head. "Livvy would never let me hear the end of it."

"That's true. How many goslings do we think we'll have this time?" As it turned out, *Ronald* was really a *Ronalda* and over the years she and Donald had proven to be quite the prolific pair. They weren't the only ones. Eleanor's collection of orphaned and beleaguered animals had grown to fill three carriage barns, part of the stables, and one room in the east wing which was dedicated entirely to hedgehogs.

Farmers and lords alike brought their sick and injured animals to Hawkridge, where Eleanor – along with a small staff dedicated solely to the care of her ever growing menagerie – lovingly tended them back to health.

"Any more than three of the little buggers and we'll have to dig a larger pond," Derek said.

"At last count there were twelve."

The duke stopped short. "A *dozen* more goslings?"

Eleanor bit her cheek to keep herself from snickering

at his incredulous expression. "Mr. Harrington has already said he would like a few. I'm sure we could convince Olivia to part with at least four or five when they're old enough to leave the nest."

"At this point I might as well put in a lake and be done with it." Derek's eyes narrowed when he saw the sudden gleam in his wife's gaze. "*Don't* get any ideas, Red," he warned. "I was being facetious."

"Of course you were," she said agreeably. "It's just that with a lake I could take in more water fowl and–"

"COME ON!" Olivia shouted, waving her arms in the air as she reached the water's edge and the thicket of cattails where Ronalda had made her nest. "THEY'RE HATCHING! THEY'RE HATCHING!"

Eleanor and Derek exchanged an amused glance.

"I suppose we better hurry," he said gravely.

Laughing, the duke and duchess ran arm in arm towards the pond and a future that was as bright as the sun.

Author's Note

I sincerely hope you enjoyed the time you spent with Eleanor and Derek! If you could take a few minutes and leave a review, I would greatly appreciate it. Every review counts, especially for indie authors like myself.

And please enjoy this sneak peek at *A Dangerous Affair*, the third full-length release in my thrilling Bow Street Bride series! Available now.

A DANGEROUS AFFAIR

A THIEF WITH NOTHING TO LOSE...
Juliet is beautiful, intelligent...and one of the best thieves in all of London. Raised in the cutthroat streets of St Giles, she's learned to survive by whatever means necessary. Even if those means include pretending to be a highborn lady to avoid capture by The Wolf, one of Bow Street's most cunning runners...and the only man to ever set her blood on fire.

A RUNNER WITH A SCORE TO SETTLE...
Grant is charismatic, titled...and second-in-command of the Bow Street Runners. When his captain orders him to find and arrest the lad who has been stealing jewelry from the ton's elite, he thinks it's just another job. Until the *lad* turns out to be a five foot, four inch red-haired hellion with a penchant for knives...and the softest lips he's ever kissed.

A DANGEROUS AFFAIR...
Juliet and Grant's daring game of cat and mouse will take them from the glittering ballrooms of Grosvenor Square to the dangerous alleys of the East End as they try to outwit one another...and fight their growing passion. But when an enemy from Juliet's past threatens her future, she has no other option except to trust the runner she has sworn to hate. Forced to choose between duty and desire, will Grant listen to his head...or risk everything to follow his heart?

CHAPTER ONE

ST GILES ROOKERY was no place for a woman after dark. Or during the day for that matter, but Juliet had never let that stop her before and she had no intention of letting it stop her tonight.

She flitted through the darkness with the fluidity of a shadow, the worn leather soles of her boots scarcely touching the ground. The black cloak she had draped over her shoulders fluttered as she turned right and then left, navigating the twisted alleys with the ease and confidence of someone who had been born into them.

Jumping over a pool of foul smelling stagnant water and piss, she stopped in front of a narrow wooden door tucked away inside of an alcove. Raising her fist, she rapped her knuckles against the door three times. Waited for the length of a heartbeat. Knocked again. Creaking on its rusted hinges, the door swung open.

"Do ye have it?" The man who spoke was old and

smelled of gin. Yet despite the map of wrinkles across his weathered face – or perhaps because of them – his watery blue gaze was cunningly sharp. "Do ye have the necklace?"

"Here." She reached between her breasts and pulled out a small velvet reticule. But when the man made a quick grab for it she shook her head and took a step back, eyes narrowing to annoyed slits of green. "How long have we been doing business, Yeti? You know I require payment first."

The old man growled under his breath, but after a moment's pause he slapped a leather pouch into her extended palm. "There," he said. "Now give me the bloody necklace."

Juliet's fingers tightened around the pouch as she tested its weight. One delicately arched brow lifted. "The rest, Yeti."

He made a scoffing sound. "I don't know what ye are–"

"The rest," she said evenly.

"Ye drive a hard bargain, Jules."

"A fair bargain," she corrected as he dug into the pocket of his sagging trousers. "And more than you deserve for the shite you tried to pull last time. Did you think I wouldn't realize those shillings were nothing more than painted copper? I should charge you twice as much for the trouble. It's a good thing we're friends,

Yeti."

"Friends," he grumbled under his breath as he gave her a handful of coins. "If I'm your friend I'd hate to see how ye treat your enemies."

"Yes. You would." After quickly counting the coins to ensure she'd been paid in full, Juliet slid them into the leather pouch and tucked the pouch into her boot before she gave Yeti what he'd paid twenty gold pounds for.

Not a bad take for a night's work, she thought silently. It would see her comfortably through to her next job, a townhouse on the edge of Grosvenor Square where another one of her buyers had his eye on a diamond bracelet.

Sliding the necklace out of its velvet pouch, Yeti held it up towards the lantern hanging above his door and whistled under his breath when the stones gleamed a deep, vibrant red. "She's a beaut, ain't she?"

Juliet's narrow shoulders lifted and fell in a careless shrug. "I suppose. I've never particularly cared for rubies."

"A jewel thief who doesn't like jewels," Yeti muttered under his breath. "What's the bloody world coming to?" Quick as a wink the necklace disappeared into the folds of his coat. In his day he'd been the best pickpocket this side of the Thames. Time and too much gin had dulled his reflexes, but his fingers were still nimble.

"Don't fancy what you take, Yeti. You taught me that." Juliet's neck abruptly swiveled when she heard the distinctive *click* of a stone being turned over. Frowning, she stared intently into the inky darkness, her hand inching down towards the knife she always carried on her waist. There was a pistol on her opposite hip. A dagger strapped to the inside of her thigh. And, just for good measure, a tiny pair of sewing shears tied to her wrist.

She'd never killed a man, but she'd spilled blood. Plenty of it. And for the past two nights she had been plagued by the uneasy feeling of being watched. But just as her hand began to curl around the smooth handle of her knife a yellow tabby darted across the alley and disappeared into a pile of wooden crates. Exhaling slowly, she turned her attention back to Yeti who lifted a scruffy white brow.

"Trouble?" he asked, scratching underneath his chin.

"Nothing I cannot handle."

"Ye could always quit, ye know. Hang it up and walk away for good. I know ye have enough blunt."

"No one ever has enough blunt." Leaning forward, she pressed her lips to his rough cheek. The grizzled old man was as close as she'd ever come to having a grandfather. Or a father, for that matter. "You taught me that as well. Sleep tight, Yeti."

"Aye." He patted his coat pocket. "With this pretty under my pillow I'll do just that. Watch yerself, Jules." A line of irritation creased his weathered brow. "The runners are getting closer. Hans said he saw one of the bastards all the way down on Finley Street. It's that damn Spencer. Never thought he'd be the one to go turncoat on us."

"Would you rather he have ended up in Newgate? Or worse?" Not too long ago Felix Spencer had been the greatest thief in all of London. There wasn't a painting he couldn't pinch. A necklace he couldn't swipe. He'd been the best...until he'd been caught. But instead of stretching him up by his neck or throwing him in prison, the new captain of the runners had given him a choice: spend the rest of his life rotting away in a cell or put his considerable talents to good use on Bow Street.

Felix had been a runner for nearly two years now, but it still gave her a jolt every time she saw him walking down the street in broad daylight. She could only imagine what it was like for Yeti. She knew the old man felt betrayed, especially since he'd been the one to teach Felix everything he knew, but what had he expected? She knew if she'd been in Felix's shoes she would have made the same decision. Anything to avoid the hell on earth that was Newgate Prison.

"He's not giving them names." She squeezed Yeti's hand. "If he were, we'd both be locked up already."

"Aye," Yeti grumbled after a pause. "I suppose ye are right about that. Still…"

"I know. It does not sit well with me either. One of our own, working for *them*." The corners of her mouth tightened. "I'd be happy if I never saw another runner for as long as I lived. Cock sucking bastards." Turning her head, she spat on the ground in disgust and Yeti chuckled.

"Easy, lass. Don't go losing that Irish temper of yours over something ye can't control."

"For the hundredth time, I'm not bloody Irish." And it annoyed her to no end every time he said otherwise. The truth of the matter was that she had no idea where – or who – she'd come from. Her parents very well *could* have been from Ireland. She had no way of knowing. They'd both perished in a fire when she was no more than a babe. To this day, she did not even know their names.

"Ye've the hair of one, don't ye? Redder than the rubies ye just pinched. Never seen the likes of it in my whole life. Fine ladies would pay a pretty penny to have that color. As would fine men," Yeti said meaningfully.

She took a step back and folded her arms. "I'm a thief, not a whore."

"And I never said ye were, did I? But ye could be a rich man's mistress. Ye have the look of one. Clean the soot off of ye face and trade those pants ye insist on wearin' for a fancy dress and ye would blend right in with all the pretty ladies in Hyde Park. Ye could live in a big house in Grosvenor Square. Have yer own servants. Go to tea parties and balls and the like. Ye could get out, lass. Start a new life for yerself."

"A mistress is just a fancy word for whore and I would rather die than belong to any man." It was not an exaggeration. The life Yeti described held little appeal to Juliet. She may not have had dresses or servants, but she was free. Free to make her own decisions. Free to do what she wanted when she wanted it. Free to live her own life as she saw fit. Could those women in their fancy dresses and big houses say the same? She answered to no one, and there was no man on God's green earth worth giving all of that up for.

"Ye say that now. Just wait until ye meet the right one. All right, all right." Yeti waved his hand in surrender when her green eyes flashed. "Don't get riled up on my account. Be safe out there, lass. Are ye done for the night?"

"I've one stop yet."

"Well best be moving on then."

Drawing the hood of her cloak up and over her head, Juliet stepped down off the doorstep and into the shadows. Skirting the pile of crates where the cat had disappeared, she walked quickly to the end of the alley. But instead of turning left as she should have done, she turned right instead and immediately flattened herself against the crumbling brick wall of an abandoned factory.

Someone was following her. She could feel it in her bones. In the whisper of awareness at the nape of her neck. In the accelerated pounding of her heart.

And it wasn't a bloody cat.

Silver moonlight reflected off her dagger as she silently unstrapped it from her thigh. A gift from Yeti, it was surprisingly light for its size with a handle made from whalebone and a thin blade that was sharp enough to carve a man's throat from ear to ear without spilling a single drop of blood.

She heard the muffled beat of approaching footsteps. A quiet exhale of breath. The rustle of fabric.

And the distinctive *click* of a pistol being cocked.

"You can come out from behind there." The voice was deeply masculine, the vernacular clear and crisp and threaded with a hint of aristocracy. "With your arms raised, if you please."

Gritting her teeth in silent frustration, Juliet lifted both arms and carefully stepped out from behind the wall. Several paces away stood a man holding a pistol. A pistol he had pointed straight at her chest. It was too dark to make out his features clearly, but his silhouette was all sharp angles and lean muscle.

She could tell he was tall. Taller than she by at least a

head, if not more. His hair was as black as the shadows that crept along the walls. And his clothes were impeccably cut to fit his lanky frame, indicating that despite his current surroundings he was a man of wealth and substance.

"Come closer," he said, gesturing her forward with a jab of his weapon.

Left with little choice in the matter, she edged forward a few inches, purposefully keeping her head tilted down. With her hair pulled back and her feminine curves hidden beneath the folds of her cloak, she passed easily for a boy. A young one given how smooth her porcelain skin was, but a boy nevertheless.

While being a female came with its own distinct advantages, there were none to be found at night in the middle of the East End. She still distinctly remembered the day Yeti had pulled her aside and asked what she wanted to do with her life. Confused, she'd blinked up at him, all wide green eyes and freckles and teeth that were still a bit too big for her mouth.

"What do ye mean?" It wasn't until later that she had taken the time to rid herself of her cockney accent, and she'd spoken with the vernacular of a common guttersnipe.

"What do I mean…" he had muttered, pulling off his cap and skimming his hand through his hair. It hadn't been gray then, but rather a thick, nondescript brown that he'd kept shorn close to his skull. "I mean ye're getting older. Taller. Ye're…filling out." His gaze had dipped down to her chest and his cheeks had reddened before he'd abruptly looked away. "Ye are turning into a woman, lass. And a pretty one at that."

"I am not!" she had cried indignantly.

"Aye." He'd crushed his hat between his hands. "Ye are. The truth is ye would have done a sight better to have been born a boy, but I guess we don't have much choice in those matters, do we? Ye are what ye are. And ye have a decision to make."

"What sort of decision?" she'd asked suspiciously before her eyes widened in distress. "Ye aren't going to send me away like you did Sam, are ye? Please don't. Please. I'll do better. I promise. I – I'll start pinching twice as many purses. And I'm ready to start on the safes. I know I am. Please don't–"

"Sam wasn't sent away, lass. She left of 'er own accord after I sat her down jest like I'm doing with ye."

"I don't understand."

"No," Yeti had sighed. "I can see that ye don't." The floorboards had creaked beneath his heavy boots as he'd walked from one side of the small, windowless flat to the other, careful not to step on the lumpy gray cot Juliet shared with Eddy and Bran, two pickpockets of a similar age. Not that any of them knew what their exact age was. They were all orphans, brought under Yeti's wing when they were still small enough to squeeze through carriage windows and take what was inside.

Sometimes, when she was very tired, Juliet closed her eyes and dreamed of a woman with soft blonde hair and a kind smile. She liked to think it was her mother, but there was no way to know for certain. Yeti and his collection of orphans was the only family she'd ever known.

"Do ye know why I always have ye wear a hat and trousers, lass?"

Juliet had nodded slowly. "So my hair doesn't get in my eyes and I can run away." Her little chest had swelled with no small amount of pride. "I'm the quickest, ye know. No one can beat me. Not even Felix."

"Aye, that ye are. But the hat and trousers serve another purpose. They make ye look like a boy," Yeti had explained when Juliet's head tilted in confusion. "Because no one bothers with boys. They're a dime a dozen around here, and no one thinks twice about them. But girls...especially girls who look like ye do...well, that's a different story. Do ye know what a lady of the night is, lass?"

"Yes," Juliet had said solemnly. "Bran told me. They let men touch their tits for money."

Yeti had snorted. "That's the gist of it, I suppose." He'd looked closely at her. "Is that something ye want to do? Let men touch yer lady parts for money? Ye would have a fine room all to yerself with a real bed. All the food ye could ever hope to eat. Silk dresses and pretty fans and fancy shoes."

"That sounds nice, I suppose." She didn't care much about dresses and fans and shoes, but she *did* like to eat.

"Ye will have to sleep with men."

"I sleep next to Bran and Eddy every night."

"Aye, but that's different. These men…they won't always be kind to ye, lass. And they'll be strangers. Strangers who use ye for yer body. It won't be pleasant work. Ye won't have a say in who comes to yer room or what ye have to do once they're in there. Do ye understand what I'm tellin' ye?"

She thought so. Or at least as much as a young girl could understand such things. "That's what Sam is now? A–" she had paused as she searched for the right word "–lady of the night?"

"Aye."

She'd chewed on her bottom lip while she had mulled it over. "But what if I want to stay here, with ye and Bran and Eddy? What if I want to be a thief?"

"If that is what ye want, that is what ye can do." Yeti hadn't said in so many words that he was pleased with her decision, but she'd known by the approving light in his gaze that she had made the right one. "I'll make ye the best thief the East End has ever seen, lass. Mark me words."

That was the last night she'd slept beside Bran and Eddy. From that day forward she had her own cot, and whenever she left the flat Yeti made sure her hair was tied back and her breasts, small as they'd been at the time, were bound flat to her chest. He called her Jules, and instructed everyone else who knew that she was really a girl to do the same.

She had been pretending to be a boy for so long that sometimes even *she* forgot she was a female. But now, standing before the stranger with his dark wavy hair and lean, muscular build, there was no doubt in her mind as to her sex.

Even without having a clear glimpse of his countenance she knew he was handsome. One of the handsomest men she'd ever seen. Just as she knew that he was trouble, and the sooner she put as much distance between them as possible the better. Unfortunately, the stranger had over ideas.

"Closer," he commanded, beckoning her forward as if she were a dog and he her master. But Juliet answered to no one, not even if they were holding a pistol, and instead of obeying his order she bared her teeth.

"Bloody hell," she snapped. "Do you want me to climb up on your lap, then? Because if you're looking for that type of service there are a few gents around the corner who would be happy to oblige. But I'm not one of them."

His husky laugh did the oddest thing to her belly. The muscles in her abdomen clenched tight and then slowly released, her insides quivering as though she'd swallowed a mouthful of butterflies. Annoyed by the distracting sensation, she shifted her weight to her toes and fixed the stranger with a fierce glare.

"What's so amusing?" she demanded.

"Your pitiful attempt at diversion. If I was after a good tupping I'd head to the nearest whorehouse. I want the necklace you stole, lad."

"I don't have any idea what you are talking about."

"Don't you?" The side of his mouth curved ever-so-slightly, as if he found her deceit amusing.

"No," she said flatly.

"Then let me refresh your memory. Lord and Lady Munthorpe reported someone broke into their townhouse four nights past and stole Lady Munthorpe's ruby necklace."

Not by a single flicker of an eyelash did Juliet betray her guilt. Being a good thief involved more than squeezing into small spaces and taking things that did not belong to you. It meant being a good liar, and she was one of the best. Lifting one shoulder in a careless shrug she said, "Maybe this Lady Munthorpe merely misplaced the necklace. Did you consider that?"

"It would be easy enough to do, I suppose," he said

thoughtfully. "Given how much jewelry she has."

"Precisely my point."

"But that doesn't explain the brooch taken from Elm Street or the sapphires that disappeared from a safe in Highland Manor, does it?"

Juliet hid her surprise behind a quick blink. How could he possibly know all that? Unless...

"*Runner.*" She hissed the word as though it was a curse, which for her and her ilk it might as well have been.

Comprised of nearly a dozen men, the Bow Street Runner's patrolled all of London and its surrounding roads and villages. Emboldened by the Crown, they were worse than thief takers and bounty hunters combined because they could not be bribed.

A thief taker you could reason with. A bounty hunter you could slip a bit of blunt to and be on your way. But a runner...a runner wasn't satisfied until the magistrate pounded his gavel. And this one in particular seemed more determined than most, for only a very brave runner – or an incredibly stupid one – would dare venture this deeply into the rotting bowels of St Giles.

Her eyes narrowed. How was it he had managed to do what all the others hadn't? She'd had a few close calls over the years, but she'd never been caught. Not by one of *them*. How long had he been following her?

Long enough to know what her last three takes had

been. Bloody hell, she hadn't even told Yeti about the sapphires. Did he know about her other jobs? Or where she lived? Her chest tightened at the thought even as a surge of anger left a bitterly metallic taste in her mouth.

Damn the runners. She wasn't hurting anyone. Yes, she was stealing, but only from those who could easily afford to lose what she took. What was one lonely ruby necklace to a woman whose husband had three carriages? Or a brooch to an estate that was nearly half the size of the East End? She could have wiped their coffers clean and there would have been no one to stop her, but she had restrained herself, hadn't she? One piece from one house; that was her golden rule. The runner shouldn't have been trying to arrest her. He should have been *thanking* her. And then going on his way to catch the *real* criminals. The murderers and the rapists and the brothel owners who employed girls as young as twelve and thirteen.

"You have no proof I stole shite," she spat.

He made a *tsking* sound. "Ah, but I do. You yourself just admitted to stealing the necklace, and as you did not deny taking the brooch I can only assume you stole that as well. You've been rather busy, haven't you lad?"

"Bollocks!" she cried. "I didn't admit to anything because there's nothing to admit to. I'm innocent."

"Is that so?"

"Aye." She gave a defiant toss of her head and met

his stare for the first time. *Emeralds*, she realized, momentarily thrown off guard when she found herself glaring into the greenest eyes she'd ever seen. *His eyes are the color of emeralds.* "You – you have the wrong person."

Bloody hell Jules, she thought in self-disgust when she stumbled over her own tongue. *Pull yourself together. Green eyes or not, this bounder is about to haul your arse down to Newgate if you don't think of something quick.*

"How old are you, lad? I suppose it doesn't matter," he went on before she could reply. "You're young yet. If you come in quietly I'll put in a good word for you with the Magistrate. He's a fair man. You'll only serve four, five years at the most. When you get out you'll still have your entire life ahead of. You can turn things around. Take an apprenticeship or better yourself through education. It's not too late."

Why did everyone think she wanted something different than the life she had? First Yeti, now this green-eyed runner who would have done well to keep his thoughts to himself. She *liked* her life. She liked what she did. She liked waking up every morning never knowing what the day would bring. Given the choice, there was nothing she would change. Given the choice, she would be a thief until she died. Which, given her current circumstances, could be any minute now.

"I'm telling you, you have the wrong person."

"I don't think so." Keeping the pistol pointed at her with one hand, the runner used the other to unclip a pair of iron manacles from his belt. "Step lively now, I've other places to be that do not include an alley in the middle of St Giles." His nose wrinkled. "Especially one that smells like piss. Honestly. How do you stand it?"

Eyeing the manacles as a wolf would a steel trap, Juliet started to edge backwards. "You can take those shackles and shove 'em up your arse, you bleedin' ratbag bastard. I'm not going anywhere with you."

"Come now, lad. Is that any way to talk to your betters?" He sighed when her hand darted down towards her waist and the pistol that was strapped to it. "Be reasonable. There's no need for violence."

"Bugger off," she said between clenched teeth. "I said I'm not going anywhere with you, and I meant it. You'll have to shoot me dead first."

His countenance softened. "No one is going to be shooting anyone. I'm not in the habit of harming children."

Well in that case…

Spinning around, she bolted out of the alley as if the hounds of hell were snapping at her heels.

Printed in Great Britain
by Amazon